D0358329

THE
BAKEHOUSE

JOY COWLEY
THE
BAKEHOUSE

GECKO PRESS

This edition first published in 2015 by Gecko Press
PO Box 9335, Marion Square, Wellington 6141, New Zealand
info@geckopress.com

Distributed in New Zealand by Upstart Distribution,
www.upstartpress.co.nz

Distributed in Australia by Scholastic Australia,
www.scholastic.com.au

Distributed in the UK by Bounce Sales & Marketing,
www.bouncemarketing.co.uk

A catalogue record for this book is available from the
National Library of New Zealand.

creativenz
ARTS COUNCIL OF NEW ZEALAND TOI AOTEAROA

Gecko Press acknowledges the generous support of
Creative New Zealand

Cover by Keely O'Shanessey, New Zealand
Typesetting by Vida & Luke Kelly, New Zealand
Edited by Patricia Lee Gauch
Printed in China by Everbest Printing Co Ltd,
an accredited ISO 14001 & FSC certified printer
ISBN paperback: 978-1-776570-07-2
E-book available

For more curiously good books,
visit www.geckopress.com

Books are created by a family. The family for this book are a wordsmith, her patient and supportive husband, wise editor Patti Gauch, designers Keely and Luke, and the great team at Gecko Press — Julia, Jane and Matariki.

— Joy

CONTENTS

CHAPTER ONE

A tall skinny boy was snooping around the grounds of the retirement village. Bert watched from his window on the upper floor as the kid investigated names and numbers on the white-painted doors. One of that gang, he thought, louts with spray cans thinking the elderly are an easy target. Need a good boot up the backside, the lot of them. This one was checking the place in broad daylight, as bold as brass. Bert's hands shook, and there was a tightness in his chest that gripped his breath. It was true an old cop never retired. All those years on the Force had rewired his brain for action. His instinct was to go down there, two steps at a time, and scare the living daylights out of the little ratbag. But his legs were useless after the long walk from the church and, anyway, the outbreak of graffiti in the village wasn't his responsibility.

He kept telling himself that. Where was the highly paid security guard who was supposed to be patrolling the place?

Bert poured boiling water on top of the tea bag, splashing over the edge of the cup because he had one eye on the window. The kid was still there, and for a second he raised his head so that Bert stared full into his face. He reminded Bert of someone, although his skin was darker, someone he knew way back – when? Hell's teeth! It wasn't only his eyesight that was shot. What had happened to his famous photographic memory? These days he would forget his own name if it wasn't in a metal frame on his door. Getting old was no picnic.

The kid had one of those crazy haircuts, shaved up the sides and sprouting on top like a rooster's comb, and he wore long trousers, some kind of school blazer. Bert's breathing got easier. Yeah. His mistake. Boy looked too respectable to be one of the graffiti mob. Probably belonged to that Tongan lady on the ground floor, still in her sixties and permanently in a wheelchair. Gangrene. Had to whack off both legs, she told him. Terrible thing, diabetes.

Now the boy was looking left and right as though he was trying to cross a street at rush hour. He was lost, that was about the size of it, standing awkwardly, the maple trees behind him, a bed of red flowers to the right. None of the upper-floor windows opened, or Bert could have called down some directions, but it was okay, the boy had worked out a solution. He turned left and pulled open the door of the Office, where Mrs Bridewell would be tapping a computer with fat fingers.

Bert flicked the tea bag out of the cup with the end of a ball-point pen, put the pen back in his pocket, and slowly carried the cup to the table beside his TV. Afternoons, he usually turned on the sports channel, but the funeral had exhausted him and he needed quiet. The silence in his unit was warm, smelling of disinfectant and last night's fish-and-chip wrappers. There were a couple of black-and-white photos near the TV, one of him and Shirley on their wedding day, and another taken when he was eleven years old, Dad's box Brownie camera, most likely: three siblings with a row of grins, Meg, Bert and Betty. He shook his head at the hopelessness of it all. Poor old Betty. She was good-looking then, quite smashing, could have been a film star given the right opportunities. Now they'd be shovelling dirt on top of her, burying a lifetime of bitterness. What a waste! It was too late to think about what-could-have-been. Anyway, the choices were hers and she'd ignored them.

He supposed he should have got a ride to her graveside service; but he didn't want to go there.

At eighty-four, he'd seen enough of cemeteries. The church had been bad enough, all those people she couldn't stand, saying what a great friend she'd been. He'd half expected the coffin lid to fly up on a mouthful of opinion. It would take him a while to get used to the fact that Betty was now silent.

Arnie had come. Bert's son had flown all the way from Whangarei for his Aunty Betty's funeral, although Bert didn't know why. Arnie and Betty had never been close. He supposed it was because Arnie liked doing the right thing, saying the right thing, a trait that his father had once found irritating. Shirley had doted on their son, and Arnie had done well enough as a high school teacher and then principal. He'd married Marama, a good-looking woman from the north, and they'd had four children, three boys and a girl, all with impossibly long Maori names. Shirley, as Irish as they came, dived right into the te reo language stuff, but Bert never got his tongue around it. English was hard enough.

The tea was too hot. He remembered how his father used to tip tea into the saucer and blow on it to cool it. Cups didn't have saucers these days, but mugs were all right. Where was he? Oh yeah, Arnie and Marama's kids. They'd all gone to university, something unheard of in his day …

The knock on the door made him jump. It'd be Stacey the nurse, checking he was all right. He licked his top lip and called, "Everything shipshape, Stacey love."

The knock came again, this time longer. Not Stacey.

"Who is it?" He didn't get out of the chair. Both of his neighbours had dementia, and Donald in unit 207 had complained that someone was pumping poisonous gas through the patterns on the wallpaper. Bert's voice got some of its old authority. "I'm busy!"

The quiet that followed was not the silence of absence but the silence of someone holding a breath. One, two, three, four, and another knock, this time barely audible and a soft voice. "E Koro nui! Ko Erueti au."

"What?"

"It's your moko Erueti."

It was Arnie's kid. His grandson! What was he doing here?

Bert tried to get out of the chair, but his legs were too weak. "Come in! It's not locked."

The door opened slowly and the tall thin boy kicked off his shoes. Crikey! No wonder he'd looked familiar. The height was Arnie's and the eyes were Marama's. Close up, Bert could see the college jacket with badges and the thick hair standing up straight as broom bristles. There was more black hair, chicken fluff, on his upper lip.

Bert struggled to get out of his chair, and fell back. He held out his hand. "You came to the funeral with your dad."

The boy smiled, and when he shook hands Bert felt bony strength. "I came with my koro. Your son Arnie is my grandfather. I am Aromaunga's eldest child."

Of course. He was far too young to be one of Arnie's brood. His great-grandson, then. "You came from Whangarei?"

He nodded.

Bert pointed to the window. "You were down there. I watched you! Didn't see you at the church, though."

The boy nodded again. "There were a lot of people at the funeral and you went very soon. I missed talking to you. Koro suggested I come here before our plane goes this afternoon. Do you mind?"

He did mind. He was tired, but it was nice the boy wanted to see him. "Of course not. Arnie didn't come here with you? Your grandfather?"

"No." The boy looked apologetic. "He's with the others."

"Well, go on then, sit down. So, you must be his oldest. Sorry. My forgettery is better than my memory. What's your name again?"

"Erueti." The boy pulled a chair out from the table and folded his long body into it. "It's a transliteration of Edward, the family name. I'm fourteen."

"Maori for Edward? I didn't know that!" Bert slapped his thigh. "My old man was Richard Edward. I was christened Bertram Edward and your grandfather is Arnold Edward. How do you spell it?"

The boy spelled the Maori version, then smiled again at the floor. "Whanau is what I want you to talk about, Great-grandfather. You know – family. I have Nanny's whakapapa, generations way back, our Maori ancestors but not Koro's. I want to learn about the pakeha side, you, your parents. Koro tells me your father came from England."

"He's wrong. It was Scotland." Bert scratched his chin. "What the heck is this all about? Some kind of school project?"

"No, it's personal. For us it is very important to know our ancestors. Koro told us you lived in Wellington during World War Two. He said you had two sisters and the oldest was Great-great-aunt Elizabeth. I never knew her. It's really strange going to the funeral of family you never met."

Bert wanted to tell him that he hadn't missed much, but that was the kind of acid answer Betty would have given, although way back then she could be as funny as a flea in a fit. Like the time their father got tough on bad language. Even *damn* was swearing. So Betty marched around the house, chanting, "Jam! Jam! Jam! Butter! Butter! Butter!" Mum and Dad knew what she meant, but they couldn't do a thing about it except shake their heads at each other and try not to smile. He picked up his tea mug. "Son, no one ever called her Elizabeth. Our mother was keen on the royal family. That's how we got our names – only they were shortened. Elizabeth was Betty, and Margaret Rose was Meg. Two princesses. Meg died when she was only twenty-four. Damnable thing. Fell off a horse. I was Bertie, the thorn between roses. Can I get you something? Tea? Water? Sorry, no fizzy drink. I'm borderline diabetic."

The boy shook his head and gave him a soft-eyed smile. "No, thank you."

Nice manners, thought Bert. Respectful. He said, "We were a very ordinary family. If you're looking for something sensational, you'll be disappointed."

The boy took a fold of white paper from his jacket pocket. "Koro said you were a detective, so you know the importance of fact-finding. Look, I've made a list of questions. You don't have to answer them all, but there are some things I really need to know. You can take your time." His voice was musical, almost girlish, but there was steel behind it. Bert wondered if he had inherited Arnie's way of wearing soft gloves to push people into obedience. "My address is at the bottom of the second page."

"Two bloody pages? That's a lot of asking." He grunted as he put down his tea. "Why do you want to know?"

The boy put the paper on Bert's lap. "You are a part of who I am. You know what Maori say? Our ancestors are the clothes our spirits wear." He shrugged. "Koro told me you were a boy during the war. I want to know about that, as well."

"The war was a bit different for us kids." Bert unfolded the paper. "Our father couldn't enlist in the army."

"Was he a peace protestor?"

"You mean conscientious objector? No, no! He was turned down for action because he had bad eyesight, a thing called retinitis pigmentosa. Blind by the time he was sixty. He worked in the Post Office."

"How did he see for a job like that?" The boy seemed surprised.

"He wore glasses. The problem with his sight was it kept getting narrower, closing down from the outside. He could see what was in front of him, but he bumped into things on either side. Once he said 'Excuse me' to a lamp post."

Erueti didn't laugh. He waited for a second, then said, "Koro said something happened during the war."

Bert felt the tightness in his chest, and deliberately made his voice light. "Oh, everything happens in a war, but children don't understand what's going on. War is the adult world and kids just have to accept it.

War news, blackouts, rationing, it was all normal to us. Everything was scarce. No imports, you see. Tea, sugar, rubber, they all came from other countries. Ships couldn't get through. You know, even now, if I see a rubber band on the street, I have to pick it up. Matter of habit."

"I'm talking about something different," said the boy. "Koro said it was a big disaster." He leaned forward and clasped his hands, long fingers already man-shaped. "I want to know, Great-grandfather. Please, tell me about the Geronimo bakehouse."

It was at that moment that Bert's elbow knocked the mug and sent hot tea over the table, his newspaper and the phone.

CHAPTER TWO

Bert didn't know why they had called it the Geronimo bakehouse. It had once been a bakery, a big brick building with ancient ovens fired by wood and coal; but when he and his sisters knew it, it was boarded up, a home for spiders and rats. As for the Geronimo bit, Bert had read nothing about the Native American chief but had been told that American paratroopers shouted "Geronimo!" when they jumped out of planes. He'd seen that in the newsreels at the flicks, men tumbling out of aircraft, dozens of parachutes opening to resemble white mushrooms in the sky. Geronimo! The word had a ring of adventure to it. Was that why he and his sisters had connected it to the old bakery? If there was a reason, he'd forgotten it. Viewed from a distance of seventy-plus years, 1943 was history soup, everything mixed up, and it was difficult to separate reality from what he had read or been told. One event, though, was crystal clear and refused to be forgotten. He'd never talked about it to the others, not Meg and certainly not Betty, but he didn't want to be buried with the truth. Someone should know what happened that winter day.

He was eleven, Betty was fifteen, and that would have made Meg about six and a half. Betty acted a lot older than fifteen and Meg seemed younger than her age. At least, that was how he remembered them. He always felt a big age space with the sisters who flanked him.

Every detail of the incident was sharp – the way the street looked that day, winter sky hard as blue ice and black shadows across the pavement, the soldiers in khaki uniforms smelling of sweat and brass polish, sun glinting on the buckles of leather belts. One soldier had a cap tucked under an epaulette and hair that stuck out his ears like hedgehog bristles. The truck was also khaki, and it seemed to be panting, the exhaust pipe blowing clouds of smoke over his legs.

The men had moved in close, a wall around him, overpowering him with their soldier smell. Four sets of eyes were so focused on him, they hardly blinked.

So he told them, and yes, he remembered it all, how the anger in his stomach unwound, filling his arms and making his shoulders ache, and how he knew, really knew in that moment, what war was about.

* * *

If history was soup, then the hillside of their home in Kilbirnie was the large pot containing all those memories. In the mix, there was a weatherboard house with a red iron roof, blistered green paint on the back door, and a white paling fence between a flower garden and the pavement. Inside the house were three bedrooms: Mum and Dad near the front door, Aunty Vi opposite, and Betty and Meg next to the bathroom. Bert's bedroom was given to Aunty Vi when Uncle Mack went to England to join the bomber squadron, so Bert had a stretcher in the little sun-porch. Dad had made the stretcher from bits of wood and sacking. It was narrow and cold in winter, but Bert liked it because it looked like a soldier's bed. Under it, he had weapons in case of an invasion, a bow cut from a willow tree and several wooden arrows with sharpened tips. He'd also made a slingshot by cutting rubber from an old hot water bottle, but the rubber was perished and there was no way of getting new stuff. Rubber came from plants in the tropics, Dad told them, and most of those islands were taken over by the Japs.

"The war will be over soon," people said. Bert

secretly hoped the war would keep going until he was old enough to enlist, then he'd have real weapons, a gun and hand grenades, and he'd be able to defend his country. It was all that he and his friends talked about.

At school, the boys crouched behind the stacked chairs in the assembly hall, pretending they were sandbags, and had pretend machine guns from sticks and bits of broom handle. *Ack-ack-ack-ack!* But at eleven, Bert was too old for that kind of game. Sometimes, he looked at the rolls of barbed wire that made a barricade on Lyall Bay beach, and he saw himself in uniform, crouched behind a gun emplacement, blasting the enemy out of the water. The landing craft would spill out hundreds of invaders, and he'd swivel the gun as they did in the newsreels. *Ack-ack!* The enemy would drop like skittles. *Pow! Pow!* Bodies littered the sand! He would get a medal for bravery, possibly a Victoria Cross, and Betty would stop talking to him as though he was a little dumb kid.

But the Geronimo bakehouse – when did they discover that? He didn't know. It was always there, further up the hill, about half a mile past their house, a derelict brick bakery in a wasteland of weeds ringed by dark pine trees. Dad had told him, Betty and Meg that if they ever went near it, he would thrash them within an inch of their lives, but he always said that and never did. They had a father who made severe threats a substitute for punishment. Mum, on the other hand, didn't mind where they played as long as they stayed together. Maybe she thought that Betty at fifteen could be trusted to look after him and Meg, although, even then, his older sister could be bossy and critical. "Bert, you are such a mess! Come here while I comb your hair!"

For a long time they simply played in the long grass that surrounded the old bakery. Betty sometimes got a Capstan cigarette from her friend Hilda at high school, and she made out she was a film star, holding the ciggy between the tip of her thumb and forefinger. But she didn't inhale. It was just a game. So what did Meg do? Bert couldn't remember that either, but supposed she picked wild flowers around the old building. She was a kid keen on flowers. He, on the other hand, was busy protecting the area with booby traps. These were simply made by tying together the tops of two clumps of tall grass, creating a loop that could catch a foot. Very effective it was, too. One day he ran into one himself, fell on some broken bricks and got a bleeding nose. When she saw the blood running down to his mouth, Meg cried in sympathy. But Bert was triumphant. He imagined a whole platoon of Huns or Japs going flat on their faces and being herded off into a prisoner-of-war camp.

It was Bert who discovered a way into the old bakery. The doors had boards over them and the windows were covered with rusty sheets of iron nailed into the frames. There was a padlocked trapdoor on the ground against one side of the building. It looked secure, but when Bert tried to lift the edge, it came up easily, leaving the piece of wood and lock behind, like a segment of a jigsaw puzzle. He propped the trapdoor against the brick wall and called his sisters. For a while they stood looking down into darkness, until their eyes gradually adjusted. They could see a dark room and an open doorway in the wall. It was a coal cellar, Bert decided, only there wasn't much coal in it. He'd drop down and see if it was safe for the girls to follow. Did Betty tell him not to be so silly? Probably. That would have made him do it. But he wasn't down there for long. The open trapdoor was the only source of light and every step took him away from it. He didn't know what was under his feet or hands, and was sure the horrible stink came from rats. Maybe they were scuttling around him. Dozens of rats! Thousands! He stopped. A narrow shaft of sunlight slanted from some high place, maybe a crack in a boarded window, but he couldn't see anything. The place was as black as the inside of a cave.

Bert knew fear was cowardly for a soldier in the making, but he couldn't stop the panic that pricked his skin and made his mouth dry. He'd read about plagues of rats. He turned to look at the trapdoor, and was relieved when Betty called down to him, telling him to come back and not be such a dozy fathead. She reached to pull him up, genuinely anxious. "You don't know what's down there."

"Not much good, anyway. Can't see a thing," he said. "We'll come back later with a torch."

They went back to the bakehouse that same afternoon, with Dad's torch, two paraffin candles and Betty's box of wax matches. In Bert's thinking, the black cave had grown beyond rats to become an Aladdin's cave of treasure. He imagined heaps of interesting garbage, tools, bowls and pans, old secret recipes. But when they all got down there with the torch and flickering candles, they were disappointed. The building was mostly empty, and what remained was useless. Everything smelled of rot and vermin. In the main room, three crumbling iron ovens with chimneys were ranged against the brick wall. He could pick large flakes of rust off with his fingernails. Nearby were wooden tables, notched, cracked, thick with dirt.

Betty shuddered. "Imagine kneading bread dough on this!"

In one of the side rooms they found two dented tin cans with wire handles, and in the other room, a few rusty storage bins, big things with hinged lids. These, too, were so dented that their lids sat up askew. There were some hooks on a wall and a leather apron hung on one. It was wrapped in a net of dirty cobwebs and none of them wanted to touch it. Meg was terrified of spiders.

"The place has been ransacked!" Betty said. "I suppose that's why they boarded it up – to prevent more people getting in."

Maybe Betty did say that. Or maybe Bert thought it much later. Whatever, it was probably the truth, and if he wrote it down, his great-grandson could sort it out.

After that, there didn't seem much point in going back inside the bakery, but they did. Many times. Why? Because it was forbidden, because it was their secret, although each time they had to make Meg promise she wouldn't say anything – she was a real blurter, that kid – and because there wasn't a lot to do in the weekends apart from an occasional tram ride to the city or the zoo.

Sometimes Aunty Vi took them to the pictures. The seats clattered when everyone stood up for "God Save the King", then clattered again as they sat down for the news – planes, ships, torpedoes and bombs! In London, the underground train stations were bomb shelters. Bert took notice of that. When enemy planes zoomed towards London, sirens went off. People ran to the underground shelters to escape the bombs. They were safe there.

In Bert's street, a siren sounded every night to warn people to put blinds over their house lights. But what if the Huns or Japs did come over? There was no bomb shelter. Only that could change! It was amazing how quickly a small idea became a real plan. When the enemy planes arrived, Bert would take his entire family to the Geronimo bakehouse. It would be their bomb shelter, and if the enemy came looking for them, they'd be tripped up by the booby traps in the long grass. Would the bakehouse be a target? Not likely! They wouldn't waste bombs on a useless old building. This plan would work. He'd clean the place and get in supplies like food and water, and once that was done, he'd tell Betty. She might be the oldest but she bossed them with stupid things, like crossing the road on the white stripes, not getting dirty, pulling up their socks – all fussy stuff that wouldn't be a scrap of use if there was an invasion. A bomb shelter wasn't stupid. Betty would be impressed.

He looked out of his sun-porch window beyond the houses that dotted the hills like postage stamps in an album. Beyond them was a wide blue sea that could hold a thousand ships, and a clear sky that could fill with enemy planes. It likely would happen. Sea and sky had an emptiness waiting to be filled with the noise of ships and bomber squadrons. With such a roaring in their ears, they wouldn't hear a warning siren. But from his bedroom window, he would see them coming. The bakehouse was less than five minutes away.

Bert huffed against the window, then wrote his initials in the breath mist. When the invasion came, he would save the lives of his family.

CHAPTER THREE

There were no men teachers at the school. They were all away, fighting to win the war. Mrs Alsop was all right, but she was old and she taught sissy stuff like art and poetry. She wouldn't let the boys draw war pictures. When Bert's friend Tim did a snazzy cartoon on the blackboard of a B-25 bomber dropping bombs on Hitler, Mrs Alsop marched down the aisle with her chalk duster and wiped it off. "We get enough of that in the newspapers," she said. "Let us remind ourselves that there are other things in this world beside war."

One time she told them to draw something in their house, and Bert copied a photograph of Uncle Mack's Wellington bomber. That wasn't cheating. The photo was on the wall in their kitchen. Bert even put Uncle Mack in the picture, standing near the leading edge of the wing, his flying helmet on.

Mrs Alsop wasn't impressed.

"It's an important plane, Miss. It was named after the capital city of our country."

She smiled then, and for a second he thought he was right. "Wrong guess, Bert. It was named after the Duke of Wellington, who won the Battle of Waterloo. Both the capital city of New Zealand, and that plane in England, bear his name."

Bert looked away. She was smiling because he was wrong. He opened his drawing pad and scribbled a row of bullets coming out of a gun. He could draw it because Mrs Alsop had broken her own rule about battle pictures. What she said was history but it was still about war, and he would tell her if she said anything. But she didn't see the picture, which was just as well. It wasn't as good as his sketch of Uncle Mack's bomber.

Bert quite liked history, though, and he was good at other things beside drawing, stuff like fractions and percentages and football. His mates in Standard Four were Alwyn, Tim and Reggie and, like Bert, they were keen to enlist. Bert wanted to be in the army and Alwyn and Reggie picked the navy. Not Tim. He got seasick, but he was dead keen on being a Spitfire pilot. Too bad they had to wait another seven years.

His friends admired Betty. Bert didn't know whether they came around after school to see him or her. "Your sister's a real humdinger," Reggie said, which was true, but who needed a bossy humdinger for a sister? If she had made them clean the bath, or polish their shoes, they wouldn't be so admiring.

Betty didn't think much of Bert's mates. She called them snotty brats, and once, when Alwyn was a bit cheeky, she said, "You're a smart fart. Who blew you?" Instead of being offended, Alwyn thought it was funny. He laughed and laughed and told everyone at school, causing Bert no end of embarrassment. Why couldn't Betty keep her big gob shut?

He thought school was a bit like the army. Not all of it, but the marching from assembly into class, left, right, left, right, to band music played on a gramophone, and then inspection, hair tidy and parted straight, hands on desk to show clean nails. Some teachers whacked your fingers with a ruler if your nails were dirty. Miss Prendergast was one of those. She used the strap a lot, too, for things like talking or throwing a paper dart. The boys called her the Sergeant Major. Compared with Miss Prendergast, learning poetry and painting flowers with Mrs Alsop was tolerable.

Bert didn't say anything to his friends about the Geronimo bakehouse. They knew it was there, all right, but didn't know they could get into it. Crikey! If he told them, that would mean the end of his plan for the bomb shelter! Soon everyone would know about it. Officials would close it off, properly, this time. They might even put an electric fence around it. Bert had felt an electric fence. That was on Reggie's cousin's farm. Reggie said you didn't get a shock if you touched the wire with a piece of wood. He was wrong. The shock belted right up Bert's arm, and Reggie nearly died laughing.

No, he couldn't tell them about the trapdoor. Sometimes he went to the bakehouse by himself, to tidy the place up a bit. Borrowing a broom was out of the question. How could you carry a ruddy big broom along the road and pretend you were going nowhere? Instead, he took a worn paintbrush from Dad's shed, tucked it with a cloth in his school bag, and used them to clean dirt off the walls and wooden benches in the bakehouse. He was careful to clean the brush afterwards. Dad didn't know he used it, but did wonder why the torch batteries had such a short life. Having only one torch in the house was a flipping nuisance. Dad was careful. He measured everything, even the life of batteries.

Bert's father was a tall, serious man who wore round glasses with brown frames and lenses as thick as the bottom of fizzy-drink bottles. Those glasses made his eyes look small. Retinitis pigmentosa was like looking down a tunnel, Dad said, and the tunnel got smaller as time went by.

Bert knew his father hated being "unfit for active service". He wore a badge that let people know he had volunteered, and he switched it between his sports jacket and his overcoat so it could always be seen. He didn't talk much about the war, but he did a lot of listening. They all listened, especially at breakfast. In the memory soup, porridge and burnt toast were mixed with voices through the radio on the shelf above the kitchen table. When Dad turned it on, it always whistled and squeaked and then settled down to music. They had their favourites. With Dad, it was the comedy chaps like Harry Lauder and George Formby. Aunty Vi and Betty liked the Andrews Sisters and Vera Lynn, while Bert preferred cowboy singers, especially Gene Autry. Now he couldn't remember any of the songs except the one they had to turn off because it upset Meg. *There's a bridle hanging in the wall, and a saddle in the empty stall, no more will he answer to my call …* Why would a kid who had never had a pony, or any pet for that matter, start bawling over a song about a dead horse? Didn't make sense.

So they'd all be sitting at the breakfast table, eating porridge, scraping toast with dripping because the butter ration had run out, Dad carefully pouring tea into his saucer and blowing on it, and it would be eight o'clock. *This is the BBC London calling. Here is the news …*

Bert knew it was coming from far away by undersea cable, because he could hear the echoes of the waves, thousands of miles of ocean licking around the words, tasting the war on them. The announcer usually sounded cheerful, as though the Allied forces were winning, but there were news items that said otherwise, the number of planes shot down over Germany, for example, and the family would avoid looking at Aunty Vi because they could feel her imagining Uncle Mack in a plane surrounded by fire from anti-aircraft guns. Being Aunty Vi, she didn't allow herself to get morbid about it. "Mack will be okey-doke. He's got more lives than a lucky cat."

Bert was sure his father didn't like his sister-in-law one hundred per cent. Aunty Vi was younger than Mum, and looked a lot like her, except Violet was noisy and Mum was quiet. As far as Bert was concerned, Aunty Vi was a good egg, fun and very generous. She worked at the confectionary counter at Woolworths, and on pay day she always brought home a bar of chocolate or boiled lollies. She'd come in the door, wiggling and singing, "Here I come, Honey-bun, I've got a paper bag full of fun," or she'd stop at the door and yell, "Who's got a favourite aunty?"

Because sugar was rationed, Mum sometimes wrapped the boiled lollies in a tea towel and crushed them with a hammer, so the crumbs could sweeten cakes and puddings. Aunty Vi knew she did this, so she brought home extra, hidden in her coat pockets. "Here, kiddos. Tuck them under your pillow."

Maybe it was Aunty Vi's friend Jean that Dad didn't like. Bert once heard his father say to his mother that Vi made herself look cheap going out with that peroxide hussy. Bert didn't know what a peroxide hussy was, and Betty wouldn't tell him.

"Dad's too serious," Betty said. "Take no notice, Bertie. There's no harm in enjoying yourself."

That was typical of Betty. She liked to make out she was grown up and knew everything, while he was a kid living in a different world.

Their father was a serious man. Every Sunday morning they had to go to church, Aunty Vi included, no arguments, no excuses. Church was deadly serious. The minister would talk on and on about how terrible the world was, and Betty would mutter it would be less terrible if he shut up. She used to take a book to read during the sermon. Dad listened to everything the minister said. At dinner he'd say things like, "Reverend Wilde made a very interesting point this morning," and "That man can be quite eloquent." But for all his seriousness, Dad liked to listen to comedians, and sometimes he made a joke. Like the time he complimented Mum for crushing the boiled lollies to get extra sugar.

She said to him, "Where there's a will, there's a way."

"No," Dad didn't smile. "Where there's a will, there's a relative."

Bert never worked out why a kind man who always saw the good in people was impatient with Aunty Vi and her friend. One rainy Saturday, Violet and Jean were in the bedroom with Betty, playing records on Vi's gramophone and teaching Betty to do the jitterbug dance. The music was loud and they were laughing, thumping the floorboards so hard that the house shook as though it was trying to dance right off its foundations. Bert and his father were in the washhouse, where Dad was polishing his shoes. Dad could have told the girls to be quiet, but he didn't. Instead he creased his face into a frown and scrubbed the shoe-polish brush across his shoes as though he was trying to peel back the leather. The music rattled the preserving jars on the shelf above the tub, glass against glass like the jars were dancing too. Dad put the brush down, the shoe down, turned around and walked out of the house in his socks. It was an odd thing to do, to walk out to the garden in the rain with socks on. Bert said so to his mother, who was peeling potatoes at the sink.

"There are odder things in the universe," she said.

"Like what?" Bert asked.

"Like grown men killing each other for reasons they don't know."

Bert's mother hated war. Mostly she was silent about it. She pulled down the blackout blinds every night, accepted rationing, stitched buttons onto underwear because she couldn't buy elastic, and made a show of being patriotic. But one part of her brain was closed off to reason and he couldn't argue with her.

"So you would just let enemies into the country?" he said. "You'd want us all to be a part of Germany or Japan?"

"That would be better than being dead," she said, calmly peeling potatoes.

Bert had been through it all before. "We didn't make this war, Mum. We have to defend ourselves, whether we like it or not! We are all in it!"

"Not all of us." She put a potato in the sink. "Women were not consulted."

How could she be so stupid? Bert wanted to tell her that she was more blind than her husband. He yelled, "Don't you realise what men are doing? They are fighting to protect women and children!"

She rinsed the potatoes under the tap. "Bertie dear, it doesn't matter whose side you are on. Every person killed in a war is some mother's child."

CHAPTER FOUR

American soldiers looked different from the New Zealand men, their uniforms a lighter colour, hats another shape. They were stationed on the west coast north of Wellington but often came into the city. They were everywhere, on trams, on the streets, in cinemas, and their voices always rose above other talking, because they were loud and kind of smooth, like they were trying to stretch the words out. It was difficult, though, to understand some accents. Bert learned new words like "Gee Willikers!" and "Doggone!" but he didn't know if these expressions were slang or not. His father didn't like slang.

Bert knew that the Americans were in New Zealand to fight the war in the Pacific. Wellington was where the soldiers relaxed before going off to the islands occupied by the Japanese. Dad was more worried by the Japs than the Germans. The Japanese were getting closer, island-hopping, Dad called it. He told Bert, "The Pacific islands are stepping stones to Australia and New Zealand. The Yanks are here to stop the invasion."

Sometimes, a truck full of American marines would come down the hill past their house, and if children were on the pavement, the men would throw them chocolate bars wrapped in gold or red paper. Candy, they called it. Occasionally, it was a pack of chewing gum and that was very welcome, because Wrigley's gum was getting scarce in New Zealand.

Once, Mum and Aunty Vi were walking out the gate when a truckload of Americans came along. The men whistled and shouted, "Hubba-hubba! Ding ding!"

Aunty Vi waved and laughed, "Hello fellas!" and Mum just smiled. After the truck had gone, they leaned against each other and laughed. "Silly boys," Mum said, looking pleased.

On a Saturday in June, Aunty Vi asked Bert and Meg if they wanted to go to the pictures in town. There was something good on, she said, a new Walt Disney film for kids called *Fantasia*. Bert liked cowboy films but they usually made six-year-old Meg cry. She didn't understand that films were not real and the arrows weren't really sticking into people. So *Fantasia* it was, and all the way in on the tram Aunty Vi told them how much she was looking forward to it. "You'll see cartoons made for the tunes of famous music," she said.

When they got there, however, Jean was waiting outside the theatre with two American soldiers. Aunty Vi said, Oh, what a surprise, fancy seeing you, and she patted down her wavy hair. Then she put her arm across Bert's shoulder. "Bert, honey, they've come all this way to see me. Here are the tickets and sixpence for a couple of big ice creams. I'll have a cup of tea with Jean and meet you outside the theatre when the film is finished. I hope you don't mind."

Bert didn't mind at all. Aunty Vi had an annoying habit of talking in a film and then asking him what she had missed. He'd been to lots of movies on his own, and, although it was a bit different taking Meg, his sister really liked *Fantasia* and didn't notice the boring bits. Bert wondered how people could get excited about dancing flowers, but near the end there was some creepy music with a mountain at midnight and ghosts coming out of graves. That was good. He let Meg hold onto his arm.

Meg got scared again when they came out after the film and there was no Aunty Vi. Not a sign of her. Bert looked at the people walking past and wondered what he should do. It would have been all right if they had money for a tram, but they'd spent Aunty Vi's sixpence at half-time, buying two threepenny ice creams.

They waited and waited outside the theatre. A cold wind swept the pavement, and it would soon be dark. Meg cried, holding onto him, asking, "What are we going to do?" He didn't know. Without money, he was helpless, and Meg would never be able to walk all the way to Kilbirnie. He thought it important that they stay outside the theatre. If they waited long enough, someone would come and find them.

They had been waiting for nearly an hour when he saw Aunty Vi in the distance, running down the street on her high heels. He knew it was her, because when she ran her legs went out sideways. As she came closer, he could see she was panting, gulping like a goldfish. Her lipstick had gone and her hair was falling down around her face. "You poor darlings! I'm so sorry!" She hugged them, pressing Meg against her skirt. "Shh! Don't cry! It's all right now. We'll get the next tram home."

There was no sign of Jean or the two American soldiers. Bert said, "That was a long cup of tea."

"Oh darling, I know, I know. It wasn't just tea. Jean's friends wanted a real meal. They took us miles and miles away to a restaurant. Oh please, my darlings, don't say anything about this. Your parents will never trust me to take you out again."

She put her arms around them and walked them towards the tram stop. "They'll think I'm the worst aunty in the world."

Bert thought that would be right. He wondered what he'd say if Mum or Dad asked about Aunty Vi being with them at the film. He also wondered how Jean and the men knew Aunty Vi was going to be there. Had that been coincidence? He didn't want to think further, because it made his stomach uneasy. He sat on one side of the tram, between an old woman and a sleeping man in a hat with the brim turned down over his face. Aunty Vi sat with Meg on the other side. His aunt took a mirror from her handbag to put on lipstick and comb her hair.

The tram swayed and rattled to the terminus and stopped. The sleeping man woke up with a grunt, and everyone got off. The sun had set and it would soon be blackout time, streets dark, no lights in any windows, nothing that enemy pilots could see from the air. The Japs hadn't yet bombed New Zealand, but they'd had a good go at Darwin in Australia, and everyone said they would get to New Zealand soon, Americans or no Americans. Covering up windows at night was very important.

As they walked up the hill, Aunty Vi made jokes about the wicked witch who had abandoned her favourite niece and nephew. "You won't say anything," she said for about the tenth time.

Meg shook her head. "No, Aunty Vi. Promise."

Bert said nothing but was feeling nervous. Actually, he didn't have to deal with any awkward questions because Mum was worried about something else. When they walked into the warm kitchen, she pounced. "Did any of you take the towels off the line?"

They stared at her, and Bert said, "What towels?"

"Two green bath towels hung out to dry," said Betty, who was doing her homework at the table.

Mum added, "I thought your father had brought them in. He didn't. Was it you, Vi?"

Aunty Vi shook her head. "I haven't touched any towels."

Mum sat in one of the chairs. "There's someone going around at night, taking stuff. Mrs Moss lost her big doormat. I mean, who would steal a doormat? She said the Hendersons lost things out of their outside room. She didn't say what. They never locked that room. My towels on the line! Oh! It's most unpleasant to know someone is sneaking around your house in the dark!"

"Are you sure the towels aren't here?" Aunty Vi asked.

"Definitely sure." Mum stood slowly and walked to the stove. "It wouldn't be a local person. People in this street are honest." She looked at them and her frown disappeared. "I suppose you're all hungry."

Meg said, "Aunty Vi—" She stopped and everyone looked at her. With a small smile, she drew up her shoulders in a long shrug and said, "Aunty Vi gave us an ice cream."

CHAPTER FIVE

Heavy rain and football practice kept Bert from the bakehouse for more than a week, but in that time his plan for a bomb shelter grew, with sketches of the old brick building and lists of stuff needed for a family of five – six if Aunty Vi joined them.

Dad's newspaper the *Southern Cross* had warnings made small to limit their scariness, but actually they were saying that invasion was close.

Reggie's father, who was in the Home Guard, said there were Japanese submarines in New Zealand waters.

"Nah!" Tim gave Reggie a friendly shove. "That's a cock-and-bull story. Our navy wouldn't allow that. They've got submarine nets all over the place."

Reggie shoved him back so that he fell against Bert. "It is so true! My father knows. He says Japanese planes have flown over Auckland."

"What a lot of rot!" Tim did not want to believe it. "You think some Zeros are going to fly over and people are going to wave and say, 'How interesting! Japanese planes!' Crap! They'd shoot them down!"

Bert listened to their argument and wondered if Reggie was right. The BBC news was all about the war in Europe, but in the bottom part of the world the Americans were fighting the Japanese in the Solomon Islands and New Guinea. Both those places were far away, but not far enough. Bert imagined Japanese ships coming south from island to island. When they reached New Zealand, what would the men of the Home Guard do, with all the fit and fighting soldiers away in Crete and North Africa? He thought a lot about this, and decided it was time he told Betty about his plans for the Geronimo bakehouse.

She was in the washhouse, ironing her gym tunic for school the next day.

"I got something to tell you." He shut the door behind him so no one else would hear. "I'm turning the Geronimo bakehouse into a bomb shelter."

"A bomb shelter?" She stopped ironing, and she didn't laugh.

"For our family. I've cleaned it up a bit, got rid of the cobwebs. Bets, it's solid brick. No one knows how to get into it. We could all hide – you, me, Meg, Mum and Dad, Aunty Vi. We'd be safe there."

"The bakehouse," she said. Then she stood the iron upright on the end of the ironing board. "For how long?"

"As long as it takes. Until our soldiers and the Americans drove them off. It wouldn't be forever. We'd stock the place with food and water."

Betty shook her head, but he knew she was considering it. "Where would we get the food?"

"When the invasion comes, we'll grab everything we can. But that won't be enough. Collecting food has to start now. I've got two cans of spaghetti."

She opened her mouth, closed it again. Then her eyes pinched into a glare. "You took Mum's green towels!"

"No! No, I didn't. I never touched those towels, cross my heart and hope to die. I didn't nick the spaghetti, either. When I come home from school, I'm hungry and sometimes Mum gives me a can of something – spaghetti, tomato soup, baked beans. Sometimes she says, Have a scone or a sandwich."

Betty snorted. "You're daft if you think Mum won't know. Where's the saucepan you used to heat it? Where's the empty can? Bertie, when you have an after-school feed, you leave a helluva mess."

"Mum's too busy to notice."

"She'll notice, all right." Betty went back to ironing her gym uniform. "It's a good idea, Bertie, but if you're serious about this, we need to make a list. The most important thing is water. At least water's not rationed. Find some empty fizzy-drink bottles and some corks. We've got pocket money. We can buy canned food, but that's useless without a can-opener – and we need candles and matches …"

He watched the iron slam back and forth on her gym tunic as she went on and on, thoughts furnishing the bakehouse. The tap over the laundry tub was dripping. He leaned against the washing machine and reached over to turn it off. It still dripped. Dad needed to fix it.

"I've got an old coat and jersey on top of the wardrobe. They could be useful, Bertie. That place is cold …"

There was no argument. He felt good about himself. Betty was dead keen on his idea.

By the time she'd finished ironing and put her uniform on a hanger, they were ready to carry their school bags to the old bakery. They had to be careful. They set the bulging bags inside the front fence, hidden by the hydrangea bush, and went back in the house to announce that they were going for a walk. It was a cold day, no rain but dark cloud and a blustery wind which gave them an excuse for not taking Meg, who was recovering from earache.

"I want to go!" she screeched. "I'll wear a hat."

Mum was not helpful. "A walk would do her good."

"No," said Betty. "She'd get tired. We're going too far."

"You're not!" cried Meg. "I bet you're going to the Geronimo—"

"Okay, okay!" Betty grabbed Meg's shoulder, then looked at Mum. "She means Jerome Street. The playground. We'll be back before five."

Bert was angry with Meg. As they walked up the hill, he said, "You broke your promise. You can't be trusted."

As usual, she started to cry. "You don't want me!"

"Too right, we don't want you," said Bert. "Does that surprise you?"

Tears flowed down her fat face framed by the purple woollen hat. "I didn't say it all. I only said the first word—"

"I know what you said," he replied. "It was deliberate. What the government says is true – loose lips sink ships! You've got loose lips, Meg!"

"Will you two shut up?" said Betty. "Now you're giving *me* earache."

They continued walking in silence, and by the time they reached the Geronimo bakehouse Meg was cheerful again. "No flowers," she said, combing the long grass with her fingers. "No daisies, no buttercups, no those little pink things."

"It's winter," said Betty. "What do you expect?"

Anxious to please, Meg forced an extra wide smile. "I like winter. I love it!"

"You're a silly fathead," said Betty.

They had not been near the bakehouse for more than a week, but the track their feet had worn in the long grass was still clearly visible and soft with the recent rain.

They opened the trapdoor and Bert jumped down first, taking from Betty the two bags. Betty lowered Meg, then got down herself, pulling the trapdoor down after her. The torch had fresh batteries and its beam was like a searchlight around the big room of the bakehouse. Bert was pleased with his work. There were still nets of cobwebs across the ceiling, but the tables and stoves were clear and most of the rubbish had gone from the brick floor. They tipped the battered kerosene tins upside down and sat on them while they unpacked the bags.

Bert no longer saw the building as a broken-down wreck. It was as familiar as home, and it seemed logical that it should be turned into a bomb shelter. There were holes in the rusted roofing iron and pinpricks of light shone through like stars from some distant galaxy, but the small back rooms were rain-proof. Sometimes, Bert thought about the men who had once worked here, cooks in leather aprons, kneading dough by hand and cooking it in coal stoves. He knew that as fact, but found it hard to form pictures in his head. His mother made bread. The same warm smell would have filled the bakery, not the stink of rat poo and mould. The rooms would be filled with light from the windows. Did they also have electric lights? He shone the torch upwards and thought that maybe the narrow pipes under the rafters were for gas lighting.

"I can't see!" said Betty. "Shine the torch here!"

She had unpacked four bottles of water and two cans of baked beans, and was now pulling out some old clothing from her bag. "We have to find a rat-proof place for these things. What about those big storage bins in the other room?"

"The lids don't fit," said Bert.

"We'll make them fit," she said. "And if we can't, we'll put the clothes in them and something on top – like an oven tray."

An oven tray! That was good thinking. Bert jumped up and yanked open an oven door. There were three trays inside, rusted, but not badly. He pulled on one and it came out with a screech. He shook off the flakes of rust. "I think this is big enough to fit over a bin."

Betty got up. "Let's see."

Bert went first with the torch, the others close behind, into the side room on the south. He waved the light about, then froze. Someone had been there! The three large storage bins were no longer in the middle of the room, but lined up against the far wall. Before he could say anything there came a deep, hacking cough from the shadows in the corner.

Bert swung around with the torch and saw a figure against the left wall. It was a man, a New Zealand soldier in uniform lying on some kind of bedding, his hand up to protect his eyes from the light.

Betty grabbed the torch from Bert and shone the beam full in the man's face. "What are you doing here?"

"It's kids," said the soldier. "Blimey! It's just kids." He spluttered and went into another fit of coughing. When he got his breath back, he said, "I thought they were coming for me."

CHAPTER
SIX

He was a young man with untidy dark hair and a soft beard sprouting on his cheeks and chin, like the fur on a peach. He'd be handsome except he was dirty and had a cold. In the torchlight, his nose was red and his breath rattled through phlegm, a noise that reminded Bert of whooping cough. It was hard to tell what his eyes were like, because he was squinting and ducking his head away from the light. He wore a regular uniform, the jacket buttoned to his chin, mittens that didn't match. Bert swept the torch over him and saw army boots caked with dried mud. The assortment of cloth beneath the man included a green towel, and there was probably another somewhere. It was all a real mess, not like a bed at all.

Betty said, "How long have you been here?"

The answer was another bout of coughing.

Betty wasn't afraid. She stepped so close, Bert thought she was going to slap him on the back to stop the cough. "You're the burglar, aren't you? You're the one who has been pinching things around these streets. Did you pinch the uniform, too?"

"No! No!" He put his hand over his face, fingers spread, the skin as dirty as his boots. "I'm not here for long. Moving on as soon as—" He coughed. "Don't say anything, eh? Please? You didn't see me!"

"You *are* the burglar!" Bert said. "That's our mother's towel."

The man twisted to yank the towel from beneath him. "Take it. I'm sorry. There's another one—" But he was coughing again, hunched over the towel and heaving as though he was trying to get rid of his lungs.

Meg said in a small voice, "I got a cold, too. I got earache."

The man fought for control, gasping between each word. "Please – don't – say – anything. They'll come – they will. They'll put me in front of a firing squad."

Bert stepped closer. "Have you run away?"

"Just one or two days. I'll go – only don't tell—" He turned his head away and coughed close to the wall, doubled up, hugging the towel to his chest.

He was running away from the army! Bert's stomach felt as though someone had punched a hole in it. A deserter! That's what he was! Deserters deserved to be shot. They refused to defend their country. Crikey! That was about as bad as being a spy for the enemy – and here was one in his bomb shelter!

When the coughing spasm stopped, Bert asked, "How did you get in here?"

"Trapdoor." The soldier wiped his mouth on the towel. "It's been bloody cold. I've got this cough. I'll go – when – just as soon as I can—"

"You're sick," Betty sounded worried. "Did you run away from your camp?"

He didn't answer.

She persisted. "You're hiding, aren't you?"

He looked towards her, blinking into the light. "Please – please—"

"What's your name?"

"Curtis. Private Donald Curtis. They'll shoot me, if you say anything. That's what they do. Stand me up against a wall and, and, I can't—" Now he was crying, a rattling, bubbling cry with snot dribbling out of his nose.

Bert clenched his fists. Deserters were worse than rats, worse than lice. They were scum!

Meg ran forward and hugged the man. "Don't cry!" she said, close to crying herself. "We won't tell. Promise."

The soldier didn't seem to notice her.

Bert stepped back, unable to find words for what he felt. The man wasn't what a soldier should be. He was disgusting, a snivelling, snotty-nosed baby, and he looked awful, as though he was going to die.

Betty brought in the kerosene tins, turned them upside down and sat on one. She lit the two candles she'd brought, put them in jars and turned off the torch. The light made their shadows dance up and down on the dark brick walls.

The soldier got his breath back and talked in a voice so soft it was hard to hear. He was Donald Curtis, age nineteen, and he had run away from Trentham Military Camp. Donald was due to be shipped out to the war in the Pacific, but he was so afraid, he had deserted. He had been living in the Geronimo bakehouse for nearly a week. "I knew the old bakery was here," he said. "I couldn't get in. Then I saw that the trapdoor to the coal cellar was a bit crooked."

Bert flinched. That was his fault. Last time, he'd left in a hurry. He hadn't set the cover exactly in place.

"I went out at night," the soldier said.

"To steal things," said Bert.

"Only things I needed. Some food. Dry socks. I didn't have a light."

Bert had difficulty sorting out what he thought. There couldn't be a crime worse than desertion, yet the bloke seemed harmless. He was really soppy, and maybe soppy blokes did get scared. This Donald chap could have had a moment of panic, run away, and then realised there was no going back. Would he be shot? Bert didn't know. In World War One, deserters were shot. Dad had told him that. In this war, conscientious objectors who refused to fight were put in a kind of prison. As punishment, they were treated badly – worse than being in the army, Dad said.

Private Donald Curtis was sitting up, holding his knees. Beads of sweat glistened on his forehead and his lips looked dry and cracked. He looked like he had a fever.

"What are you going to do?" Bert said.

"I told you – when I'm better, I'll go. I – I got wet hiding in the bush. Freezing cold! I don't want to be a nuisance."

"Where will you go?" asked Bert.

"I've got an uncle in the South Island. Good bloke. He wouldn't turn me in. He works on a sheep station. I reckon I could hide out there until the war is over." He looked at them, then said, "What about you?"

"What about us?"

"You live in the house with the towels. What are your names?"

Betty took over. She told him their names, ages, their classes in school. "You're very sick. You need some cough mixture," she said in her bossy voice. "We can get you some. Have you got food?"

He waved a hand at the bins against the wall. "Two packets of water crackers, some apples and a jar of peanut butter."

"Stuff you pinched?"

He didn't answer.

Bert wanted to take back the words. Heck, he wasn't really a deserter, not someone deliberately betraying his country. He'd got scared, that was all. He'd made a mistake and now there was no going back. Bert shrugged. "We've got two tins of baked beans you can have, but no can-opener. You got a pocket knife?"

"Yeah. It's got a can-opener on it."

"That's okay. We'll leave you the beans and the candles. And the matches."

"You won't tell anyone?" Donald Curtis looked as though he was going to cry again. "You honestly won't?"

"No," said Bert. "We won't tell anyone."

Betty folded her arms. "How did you get here?"

"Walked. Three nights. Over the Rimutaka hill in the dark. I had to hide in the bush when it was light." He coughed again. "It rained a lot. After the hill it was a railway shed in Lower Hutt. I remembered the old bakery here." The spasm overwhelmed him and he doubled up again, clutching his chest.

"That sounds like whooping cough," said Betty. "I'll come back with cough medicine."

He was wheezing too much to answer, and they had to leave.

As they climbed through the trapdoor, Bert said to Betty, "How are you going to get cough mixture?"

She rolled out of the opening, stood up and brushed down her skirt. "There's some in the medicine cabinet at home, a full bottle of Bonnington's Irish Moss."

"Mum will know if you take it," he warned.

"I'm not taking it," she replied.

"Huh?" He stared at her and she gave him her mind-your-own-business smile.

She wasn't speaking in riddles. That same afternoon, his sly sister tipped the dark cough mixture into an empty jam jar, and then smashed the empty Bonnington's bottle on the concrete path. After she had picked up the glass and hosed the concrete down, she went in to Mum and apologised for being clumsy.

"We'll take it to him tomorrow," Bert said.

"He needs it now," she said, and that same afternoon she went back to the Geronimo bakehouse with the jar of cough mixture in her bag.

CHAPTER SEVEN

Bert didn't know what to think about the soldier being a deserter. Well, he was one, but a deserter by accident, sick and scared. Bert and Betty whispered about ways they could get food to him. Since it was Betty's job to make the school lunches each morning, it would be easy to put an extra sandwich in each. "Not Meg's lunch, though." Betty grinned at her brother. "That would be oh so risky. She'd probably tell Mum that she forgot and ate Donald's sandwich."

They could keep leftovers, again Betty's idea, a simple matter of having a jar or tin can in their laps while eating dinner, and of course, there was the vegetable garden. Bert looked at Dad's garden, but the only plant that was okay uncooked was celery. No tomatoes. No sweetcorn. No green peas. He wondered if the soldier could eat raw cabbage.

Nope. Only caterpillars ate raw cabbage. But a few stalks of celery wouldn't be missed.

Nearly everyone in the street had dug up their lawn to plant vegetables. 'Dig for Victory' was on billboards everywhere, and in newspapers. It was the slogan on packets of seeds. That's what Dad did – dig, rake, fertilise, plant. But vegetable gardens sulked in winter, and now there wasn't much choice. The second night, they took the soldier a meal of two sardine sandwiches, a meat patty swiped off Bert's plate, a spoonful of bread pudding and two stalks of celery.

They didn't have to worry about water, though. Donald told them there was water connected to the tap over the sink in the big room of the bakehouse.

"No, there isn't," said Bert. "I tried that tap – a couple of times."

"I turned the water on at the mains," said Donald.

"Mains?" Bert was puzzled. "What mains?"

"Out on the footpath. There's an iron plate. Lift it and underneath is a round tap. It's called a toby."

"Oh that! I forgot it was there." But the truth was Bert had not known what a water toby was, and he felt both annoyed and pleased. The Geronimo bakehouse bomb shelter would have running water. There was, however, a new concern. Suppose the invasion came soon and they had to go to the shelter. How could they explain Donald to Mum and Dad?

"How long will he stay there?" he asked Betty.

"Until his cold is better," she said.

"But how long will that be?"

"As long as a piece of string!" She gave him a shove. "Do you think he likes living in the bakehouse?"

He pushed her back and ran out of reach. "Of course I don't. I just asked—"

"You heard him. Soon as he can, he's going to the South Island to his uncle's farm."

"How?"

Betty tossed her head, making her hair fly out like a curtain in the wind. "I'll work something out."

It was also Betty who suggested that they take turns after school to visit the bakehouse, so that one of them could be at home with Meg, who was the weak link. It was true that she couldn't be trusted. At the table, she had said to them in a loud whisper: "I'm not telling anyone. It's a secret, isn't it? The soldier is a secret." Just as well Mum had been talking to Dad about a new element for the electric jug. If they'd heard it could have been the end of everything.

One afternoon, Bert was helping Meg to sound out her letters. She wasn't a fast learner, and she couldn't grasp that a letter on its own had one sound, and in a word, another. He went through the alphabet with her. "Ay sounds like a for apple. Bee sounds like b for bed."

"B for bed," she echoed.

"Cee sounds like c for cat. Dee sounds like—"

"D for Donald!" she said, laughing and clapping her hands.

Mum was in the room and Bert had to be quick. "That's right. D for Donald Duck. Quack, quack! All right, let's draw some ducks with your crayons."

When Dad came home from the Post Office, he said that the burglar had struck again. "I was sitting on the tram with Ernie Hetherington. He had the petrol taken out of his car last night."

"Oh dear!" Mum looked anxious. "I suppose it could have been someone with a desperate need. A week's ration of petrol is so small. How far can anyone go on two gallons?"

"He's not the only one." Dad took off his hat and coat. "There's a family at the bottom of the hill. They've got that 1936 Austin 10 parked outside. You want to see it now. It's propped up on four stacks of bricks and the wheels are missing. Don't know how our burglar managed that, unless he had a jack."

"It might be a different burglar," Bert suggested.

His father shook his head. "There's money in tyres. I don't know what the world's coming to. All this theft, people buying and selling on the black market – where is the honour, hmm? Our boys are dying over there, giving up their lives for this country, and here people are using the war for personal gain. It makes you despair for the human race."

Despair. It was such a serious word that it made Bert feel heavy. He thought about fear and how it could cause a terrible situation that didn't allow you to correct the mistake. There was no going back. You just went on and on getting deeper in trouble. That kind of despair was like sucking quicksand. That's where Donald was. In quicksand. Someone had to help him get out.

Mum put her hand on Dad's back. "Dick love, it's shepherd's pie tonight – and some of your nice Brussels sprouts."

He turned to her, his eyes far away behind his thick glasses. "Women have an amazing capacity for trivia," he said, and walked out of the kitchen.

"He's in a grumpy mood," Bert remarked.

"Don't say that!" His mother's voice was sharp. "You have no idea how it hurts your father that he can't be over there."

Bert was surprised. "But you don't believe in war!"

"I'm not talking about me. I'm talking about your father." She pushed a handful of cutlery at him. "Set the table!"

That night Betty whispered, "I'm worried, Bert. Donald's still got his cough."

"I thought he looked better," Bert murmured.

"His fever's gone, but the cough is simply awful. It's been six days. He's finished the mixture. I have to get him some aspirins and honey and lots of lemons."

"How?"

"The Fosters have a lemon tree in their greenhouse."

"No! Bets, you can't!"

She smiled. "Oh Bertie! They'll just blame the burglar."

The next afternoon it was Bert's turn to take supplies to the Geronimo bakehouse. His bag was full, a jar of meat and potato, Brussels sprouts, a slice of steamed pudding, six aspirin tablets folded in lunch-wrap paper, half a jar of honey, and a heap of stolen lemons. Betty had got the lemons in the middle of the night, a stupid trick. If she'd been caught, people would think she was the burglar and she might even end up in Borstal. Even worse, someone might stop Bert on the road and ask him what he had in his pack. He was innocent, yet he was carrying stolen goods.

It was a relief to pull up the trapdoor of the bakery and drop down inside.

Donald had one candle burning. He was careful with the candles, he said, he needed to make them last, so he burned them only for a short time each day. "My eyes get used to the darkness," he told Bert. "It's not one hundred per cent dark. The light that comes through holes and cracks is enough for me to feel my way around. What have you got?"

Bert unpacked the bag. "Betty says you're still coughing. This is supposed to fix it. You mix aspirin, honey and lemon juice."

But Donald was shovelling food into his mouth, first the meat and sandwiches and then the pudding, spilling crumbs into his whiskers. Bert realised that one small meal a day wasn't enough, and somehow they'd need to find more food.

The soldier had set himself up well in the bakery. There was a spade in the corner, another stolen article, most likely. In a place where the concrete floor had been cracked, slabs of concrete had been levered up and a hole dug in the earth.

"Latrine," Donald said.

Bert had not thought of that, either, in his planning of the bomb shelter. Of course, people had to go to the toilet.

Donald told him how he had found the way into the building that first night, thanks to Bert's carelessness with the trapdoor. "It was dark. Couldn't see a thing, but it was better than being out in the rain." He ate the last bit of steamed pudding. "So you reckon this'll be your bomb shelter?"

"Yeah. That's why we had those cans of baked beans that first day."

"Sorry I ate them." He ran his fingers through his hair. "One day I'll pay you back. Honest to God

I will – when all this is over. I don't know where I'd be without you kids."

Dead, Bert wanted to say – but did people die of bad coughs? Not as dead as with a firing squad, that was certain. Betty was right when she said Donald must stay in the bakehouse until he was better, but he hoped that would be soon.

"Did you tie up the grass outside?" The soldier was smiling.

"What?"

"The long grass. Was it you?"

"Oh yeah. Booby traps."

"Gee whizz!" Donald laughed and the candle flame flickered. "That explains it. I was the booby. You got me twice. My boot caught in the loop and over I went. First time, I didn't think too much about it. Second time wasn't coincidence, so I felt around. There are dozens of the bloody things."

Bert was pleased, especially since Betty had told him his traps wouldn't work. He told Donald that he shouldn't go out at night. "People still blame you for things stolen – petrol, the tyres off cars, all sorts of stuff. Be careful. You get blamed for every crime."

"Burglary is nothing," said Donald. "A year in the clink. What's that compared with getting shot?" He began to cough.

Bert noticed that he was wearing Betty's old Fair Isle jersey under his khaki jacket. "You don't want to get caught," he said. 'When you get better, we'll find some clothes for you, civvies so no one'll know who you are. Betty has some ideas about getting you to the South Island. She thinks she can get money for your ferry ticket—" He stopped. "Are you all right?"

He obviously wasn't all right. The cough went on and on, using up his breath. When he stopped, he was quivering with exhaustion. "Sorry," he said.

"You have to get better," Bert leaned closer. "You got a mother and a father?"

Donald didn't answer, and Bert wondered if they were dead.

"Me and Betty, we've been thinking – apart from the army, who will be wondering where you are? There must be someone."

The young soldier shook his head, but it was such a small shake, it could only be half the truth. "You haven't told anyone I'm here?" he said, his voice thin with suspicion.

"No. No one," said Bert.

"What about the little kid – Meg. She hasn't said anything?"

"No." Bert picked up his empty bag. "I swear to you, cross my heart, nobody but us knows. Look, we'll try and get you enough food. Just remember, people are looking for the burglar. Don't go out. Promise?"

Donald looked as though he was going to cry again. "Yeah. Promise."

CHAPTER EIGHT

Their routine of bakery visits didn't arouse their parents' suspicion, because neither Betty nor Bert was in the habit of arriving home from school before five o'clock. There had always been extra basketball or footy practice, a library visit, time with friends. Meg was still in Primer Two and she got out early, so she and her friend Esther walked home with Esther's mother. Bert and Betty took turns going to the Geronimo bakehouse, one carrying food to Donald while the other stayed with Meg to make sure she didn't give the show away. Mum and Dad saw nothing unusual.

It was Aunty Vi who knew something was up. One afternoon, she cornered Bert and Betty in the hallway. "What are you kids up to?"

Bert shrugged. "Nothing."

"What do you mean?" said Betty.

Aunty Vi's eyes narrowed with suspicion and laughter. "I see you squirrelling half your dinner into little pots. Midnight feasts? Stray dog?"

Bert looked at Betty, who said quickly, "Stray dog."

"Okey-doke." Aunty Vi tilted her head and laughed. "You don't want to tell me, fair enough. But here's a couple of extra chocolate frogs in case your dog eats chocolate." She put in Betty's hand a white paper bag containing two chocolate frogs filled with peppermint cream.

Afterwards, Bert accused Betty. "You told her!"

"I did not!" Betty looked along the hallway, although Aunty Vi had long gone. "She might have guessed."

"How?"

"One and one make two, little brother. A burglar is nicking food and towels. And then there's the rumour about a Kiwi soldier hiding somewhere in this area." Betty folded her arms. "Aunty Vi doesn't know, but she has suspicions. I think she's trying to warn us to be careful."

"But she doesn't know where he is. I mean, she hasn't guessed." He tried to read Betty's face. "Has she?"

"No." His sister smiled, reached out and ruffled his hair. "No one would guess where in a hundred years."

The stray dog suggestion stayed with Bert. He thought about it the next day at school, until it grew into one of those practical ideas. In the middle of the playground was an empty petrol drum that served as a rubbish bin. At lunchtime, the kids threw their lunch wrappings in it, as well as any food they didn't like. Bert felt he wasn't exactly lying when he walked past the kids who were unpacking their lunches. "If there is anything you don't like, can you put it in here for a stray dog?" He held out a brown paper bag.

Alwyn was curious. "What stray dog?"

Bert thought of Donald doubled up, coughing. "He's skinny and sick. I'm trying to feed him."

Isobel opened her lunch, peeled back some brown bread and sniffed. "Would he eat Marmite sandwiches?"

"He'd love Marmite sandwiches."

"Good." She tipped four sandwiches into the bag.

Bert knew that Betty would be impressed.

Another kid said she hated fish paste, and the girl next to her wasn't keen on luncheon sausage. Alwyn's grandmother had given him a slice of fruit cake but he'd dropped it on the concrete. He wiped it on his shirt and gave it to Bert for the bag.

"Are you going to keep the dog?" he asked.

Bert shook his head. "I told you, it's a stray," he said. "It's wild." He put the fruit cake in with the sandwiches. It looked clean enough. As Aunty Vi always said, what the eye didn't see, the heart didn't grieve over.

Because Betty liked being in charge, she was now doing most of the visits to the bakehouse. Bert had collected a bag full of food, and he thought he should take it to the soldier, but Betty wanted to go. "Give it to me!" She held out her school bag and flicked open the lid. In it was a comb and Mum's good sewing scissors. Bert stared, not quite believing his eyes. She saw his hesitation and leaned forward. "Forget it!" she said in his ear.

"I didn't say anything."

"You were going to."

Bert tried to keep his voice quiet. "You can't give him Mum's scissors!"

"I'm not giving them to him! I'm just going to trim his hair."

He didn't understand. "Why?"

"Because it needs trimming, fathead!" She laughed. "Put the bag of food in before Mum comes along."

"I want to go with you."

"You can't."

"Why not?"

"Because it's your turn to be with Meg." She closed the lid on the bag and clicked the clasp. "Go on, Bertie, be a sport."

"What if Mum asks about her scissors?" he said.

"She won't. And she knows I've got basketball

practice." She laughed and messed up his hair, something she did when in a good mood. "Don't scowl, little brother. The food is a cracker idea. You've got initiative, I'll hand you that."

He wanted to go with her. When she walked out through the back door, she left an emptiness he could not explain. It was as though she had taken the air out with her and made it difficult for him to breathe. Scissors? Why? Did Donald really want his hair trimmed? It could be Betty bossing him the way she bossed Bert. Or was it something else? Bert's stomach felt squeezed tight, like when there was a spelling test and he hadn't learned the words. He went into the living room where Meg was sitting on the rug in front of the fire, playing with paper dolls. She had lined them up on the rug and was singing to them.

"Bless them all. Bless them all, the long and the short and the tall. They'll get no promotion this side of the ocean. So cheer up my lads. Bless them all."

Then she picked up the paper dolls and threw them towards the fire. Some disappeared in a lick of flame. Others landed on the hearth and curled with the heat.

Bert gasped. "Meg! Why did you do that?"

"They got deaded in the war," Meg explained.

CHAPTER NINE

That Friday night, Aunty Vi did not come home. The telephone rang at about seven o'clock, and Dad answered it. He came back to his chair by the fire, tapped his finger on the arms, and stared into the fire, orange flames reflected on his glasses. After a while he said to Mum, "She's not coming home. She's staying in town with Jean."

"Oh." Mum put down the sock she was darning. "In that case, I'd better take her dinner out of the oven."

As she stood up, Dad said in the same tone, "Does Mack know about these goings on?"

Mum glanced at Bert, then said, "There are no goings on, Dick, and you know it. Jean has been her friend since schooldays. Oh gosh, I remember when they used to play hopscotch together. When was that? Eighteen years ago?"

Dad grunted and stared at the fire, but not for long. Meg ran to him and climbed up on his knee. "Tell me little Meg pig, Daddy."

He looked at her and his face softened. He took off her slippers and, beginning at the big toe of her right foot, chanted, "This little pig went to market. This little pig stayed home. This little pig had roast beef. This little pig had none. And this little pig was called Meg—"

She squealed in anticipation and put her head down to hide her neck.

His fingers marched up her leg, over her stomach and chest, and burrowed into the closed neck. "–and Meg went wee, wee, wee, all the way home."

She wriggled, helpless with laughter. "Do it again, Daddy!"

"No, I'm tired."

Please, pul-lease!"

He started on the other foot. "This little piggy went to market …"

Bert got up to help Betty in the kitchen. It was their turn to do the dishes. Mum had covered Vi's dinner with a plate and was putting it in the meat-safe to keep cool while Betty stood at the sink, scrubbing the saucepans. The rest of the dishes were stacked upside down on the bench, waiting for Bert and a tea towel. He had barely started drying them when Dad came through from the living room. He leaned against the doorway and said in a light but careful voice, "Meg says she has a secret she can't tell me."

Bert went still, the tea towel flat against a dinner plate. Betty rinsed a pot under the tap. "Don't be so nosey, Dad!" She smiled at him. "Hasn't it occurred to you it might just be something to do with your birthday?"

He put his hands up, palms facing them, and stepped backwards. "Sorry! Sorry! Me and my big mouth!"

Which wasn't true, Bert thought. Now, Reggie's dad, he had a big mouth, and the school principal, Mr Grimshaw, he could talk until the cows came home. Not Dad, though. If he said something, it was because he thought it was important.

As soon as he had gone, Betty dropped the saucepan back in the sink and put her arm out to Bert in a gesture that was half hug, half pat. "You finish up here. I'll put Meg to bed," she murmured, her eyes alert with warning.

"She's going to spill the beans," Bert whispered back.

On Saturday morning, Aunty Vi wasn't back for breakfast. No one mentioned it, but the gap at the table said a lot. Meg stirred her porridge and dreamily recited, "Heil Hitler, yah, yah, yah. What a nasty little man you are. You eat your porridge with a knife and fork. Heil Hitler, yah, yah, yah."

"Do shut up, Meg!" said Betty. "You're such a little gasbag."

"That's not very nice," said Mum, which was a signal for Meg's eyes to fill with tears.

There could have been a crying session but for the knock on the back door. It was very loud – a hammering, more like it – and Bert's first thought was that something had happened to Aunty Vi.

Dad opened the door, and they saw two men in uniform. They didn't appear to be regular soldiers. Together they filled the doorway.

"Good morning." One held out a card. "Sorry to disturb you, sir. We're military police conducting a search in this area. We are looking for a missing serviceman."

CHAPTER TEN

The men were polite but unsmiling. They came into the kitchen and showed Dad a piece of paper that contained their authority to search, and a photo of someone who, even from a distance, was obviously Donald Curtis. Bert concentrated on his porridge, although he wanted to see how Meg was reacting. If she said anything, they'd be in deep trouble. She was silent, and Bert saw later that Betty's hand was under the table, holding her sister's hand in a firm grip.

The kitchen lost its warmth with the back door wide open, but none of them got up to close it. The men acted as though the house was theirs, and walked through to the hall in their boots, opening and shutting doors. From the banging, Bert thought they could be looking in cupboards and wardrobes, but he wasn't sure. The family had stopped eating, and the cold morning air settled over the table and their breakfast.

Bert glanced at Betty and saw that her cheeks were flushed red and her mouth was thin. He knew she was scared. Bert wanted to tell her that they would never find him in the Geronimo bakehouse. It was the one place where he was safe.

The men came back and asked Dad if his shed was locked. It was. He took the key off the shelf and went out with them, came back on his own. "They're very thorough," he said. "They looked in the shed and now they're groping around under the house."

"What nonsense!" Mum said. 'What a silly waste of time!" She tuned the radio to 2ZB and turned up the volume to hide the sounds that came up through the floor, but moments later she had to turn it down again. The men were at the back door again, patting dust off their uniforms. They had questions. Have any of the children seen this man? The photograph was passed around the table. Bert and Betty shook their heads. Meg looked at the men with big blank eyes, and said, "Nope."

The man with the small moustache said, "We believe he's in this area. There have been reports of theft. Apparently this house had something taken."

"Two towels," said Mum. "Hardly the King's treasure."

"Exactly," said the other man. "Didn't it seem strange that a burglar would take towels? Was there anything else missing? Foodstuffs? Clothing?"

"Not that I know of," said Dad.

"Two green towels," said Mum, folding her arms.

"Righto, lady," said the man with the moustache. "On to the next place." He held out his hand to Dad. "Sorry to interrupt your breakfast. We'll catch the little bugger, no doubt about that. He'll be hiding in someone's garage or shed. It's only a matter of time. If you see or hear anything, get in touch."

They left but didn't go far. The army Land Rover was parked further down the street, and Bert thought they would probably search the area all day. They couldn't risk going to the Geronimo bakehouse.

He and Betty stood by the front gate. "He'll be hungry," said Bert.

"Don't think so," said Betty, leaning over the gate to look at the Land Rover. "You got him a heap of food yesterday. There'll be some leftovers."

He turned to her. "Did you bring back Mum's scissors?"

"Of course I did."

"Did you—?" He didn't know how to say it.

"Did I what?"

He scraped at a blister of paint on the gatepost. "Cut his hair?"

"Cripes, Bert!" She was angry. "What's eating you?"

"Nothing."

"Well, belt up, then. The military police won't be around when it gets dark. I can find my way at night."

"You're going to see him?" He was alarmed. "But what if they're out tonight? They think night-time is when he comes out of hiding. Bets, they'll catch you!"

"But he doesn't come out at night," said Betty. "Not now. If they are watching, it'll be around these houses. I'm not stupid, Bert. There's no law says I can't be out on the road at night – as long as I don't have a torch. If I see or hear anything, I'll just keep walking."

"Will you take him food?"

"Food and more soap."

"You already took soap."

"Laundry soap," she said. "Do you think I'm going to bring back his shirt and underwear and socks and wash them in Mum's tubs? Huh? Hang them out on the line?"

"No."

Betty threw open her hands. "Well then! What's the problem?"

"Nothing." Which was true. But something was bothering him, although he didn't know what it was. It was somehow connected with the idea that Betty knew a lot more about Donald than he did. Cutting his hair? Talking about his underwear and socks?

A few hours later, Aunty Vi came home, as chirpy as a parrot. She and Mum talked in the kitchen, but Dad walked out of the house to work in the shed. When Mum went to the front of the house to do the vacuum cleaning, Bert slipped into the kitchen. Aunty Vi was sitting at the table, having a cup of tea. Her hair looked posh, rolled up on her head, and she had on a red jacket with wide shoulders. "Hi, kiddo," she said. "I heard you had some visitors."

"Oh yeah. They were looking for the burglar." He smiled. "Aunty Vi, I was wondering. Last night Mum put your dinner in the meat-safe. Do you want it?"

She folded her hands, put her chin against them, and gave him the longest stare. "For you or for that stray dog?"

"Huh?" He felt his face get hot.

"Listen, buddy, I don't want to know. Understand? So don't tell me any details. Of course you can have my dinner. But I'm thinking your stray dog needs more than cold curried sausages. He needs a new home somewhere else. I'm going to give you your birthday present in advance." She undid a button on her jacket and reached down the front of her dress, drawing out a small cloth purse. She opened it and took out a note.

"One pound!" he cried. "Oh, no! Aunty Vi, I–"

"Shh!" She put her finger to her red lipstick mouth, and then pushed the one-pound note into his hand. "A birthday present, remember. Tell Betty she can get her birthday present early, too, but be careful, kiddo. You children must be very, very careful. Stray dogs can be dangerous."

CHAPTER ELEVEN

Sunday afternoon, they took Meg to the children's playground, and while she was playing on the swings and slide they discussed the money. Betty said, "Aunty Vi's right. He needs to go where he'll be safe. If the military police are searching for him, they could get to the bakehouse."

"They can't get in," Bert said, but he knew they probably could. Nailed-up doors wouldn't stop them.

Betty took the two one-pound notes out of her pocket. "This will get him civvy clothes and a ticket on the ferry."

Bert wasn't so sure. "It might cost more than that."

"We'll get the clothes in a second-hand shop. They'll be no more than a couple of shillings. I can find out how much the ferry is."

It sounded all right, but Bert had a mind that searched for cracks and flaws. "If he's in civvies, people might want to know why he isn't in the armed services."

"Donald looks young." Betty waved to Meg who was at the top of the slide, yelling at them to look at her. "With his whiskers shaved off, he could pass for sixteen, too young to go to war. We'll give him some glasses so he looks like a student. I think he can do it, Bertie. He's got this uncle who works on a sheep station way up in the hills in Central Otago. No one would find him there. He'll sign his letters with another name."

Letters? Bert looked at her. "He's going to write to you?"

"Oh yeah." She smoothed her skirt over her knees. "We want him to keep in touch, don't we?"

"What if the military police start checking our mail?"

"Why would they?"

He shrugged. "For the same reason they've been searching houses."

Betty laughed at his anxiety. "He'll have a different name, Bertie."

Bert felt something inside him that was as heavy as an unexploded bomb. He didn't know what it was, but it made him speak very carefully. "Why do you want to write to him?"

She laughed and pulled his head against hers. "Stop worrying, Bertie! Anyway, he can't go yet. Not while they're looking for him. He thinks it will die down, and it will. This war is a whole lot bigger than one missing soldier."

Bert asked, "How long?"

"We don't know. Until it gets quiet, I suppose. Maybe another week? One good thing, his cough is getting better." She pulled away and gave him her sly grin with one eyebrow raised. "Thanks to the Fosters' lemons."

Bert leaned forward, looking at his hands. "Do you think it's true about the firing squad? Will he really get shot if they find him?"

"Yeah, I think so. They shot deserters in the last war." She bit her thumbnail. "He's really, really scared about that."

"Then why the heck did he run away? I mean, if he knew that, why did he take the risk?"

She shrugged. "I don't know, but I reckon Donald's chance of getting away with this is better than his chance of being shipped off to the islands and killed by the Japanese."

Bert had more questions, but the conversation ended because Meg wanted Bert on the end of the see-saw. Because he was heavier than Meg, he had to sit further up the plank, his hands behind him on the iron handles. He still went down with a thump that lifted her off the seat. She shrieked with laughter. "Again, Bertie! Again!" Bert sighed. He was well past playground games, but her face was lit with happiness and she stretched her arms. "I love you this much, Bertie." Mum was right when she said Meg was an angel.

When they arrived back home, the kitchen was empty. The tea wasn't cooking. Dad was down in the shed and Mum was in the living room with Aunty Vi and Jean. Bert heard their voices through the wall. He put his head around the living room door and saw Mum is her usual chair, and Aunty Vi with her friend Jean on the couch. The fire was going, burned down to embers. When he pushed the door open, they all turned their heads to look at him, and he realised that Jean had a handkerchief to her face. She had been crying.

His mother frowned at him and he promptly backed out, closing the door. He knew what had happened. It would be his father. Dad had said something to Jean that had upset her.

He went back to the kitchen where Betty was making a secret Donald sandwich stuffed with cheese and pickle. "Jean is crying."

"Yeah?" Betty looked surprised.

"I don't know why Dad is so mean to her …"

Meg heard him and said, "Daddy's not mean. Daddy's not mean. Daddy's not—"

"Shut up, Meg," said Betty. "Of course Dad's not mean. He's just a bit old-fashioned in his ways. If they're stuck in there, I suppose we'd better put the tea on. What do you want? Scrambled eggs on toast? Meg, you make the toast. Bert, be a nice brother and set the table. And get the slop out of the meat-safe."

Bert opened the chiller cupboard in the wall. Slop was what they called their mother's attempts to make the butter ration go further by melting the butter, adding milk and whipping it all into a pale solid mass. He took out the cutlery and set the table. Should he set a place for Jean as well as Dad? He didn't know.

Before the eggs were ready, they heard the front door open and close. Jean had gone. He breathed deeply in relief, and finished the table with the usual place settings, and on each dish he put a slice of slop toast.

Dad came up from the shed and washed his hands in the tub in the washhouse. He sat down, looked at them all, and then said grace. "For what we are about to receive, may the Lord make us truly thankful, Amen."

During the meal he talked about the military police and their search for the deserter. They were going to every house that had reported something stolen, he said, and they were putting a photo of the man in shop windows.

Photos? Bert sat up straight, but he didn't look at Betty or his father. Somehow photos made it all very serious, like Donald was a dangerous criminal. He glanced across the table at his mother and Aunty Vi, but their faces had not changed. Had they heard what Dad had said? They were quiet tonight. Maybe they were thinking about Jean's visit.

Bert thought Jean was a nice lady who usually laughed a lot. She had yellow hair and slightly bulgy blue eyes, and she put brown paint on her legs instead of stockings. Dad had no right to make her cry. Bert didn't know how a religious man like his father could do that.

Bert was in bed, reading a comic, when Betty came into his sun-porch. "You're wrong about Dad. He didn't say anything to Jean."

"She was crying," he said.

"Yes, but it was something else. She was upset. She came to talk to Aunty Vi, and Mum talked to her too."

He closed the comic. "What was wrong?"

"She's pregnant," said Betty. "She's having a baby."

"What?" He frowned. "She can't be! She isn't married!"

Betty slowly shook her head. "Bertie, you think you're a smart kid, but what you know would fit in a sparrow's eye."

CHAPTER TWELVE

What Alwyn and Tim had said about babies was very different from his father's talk about marriage and family, and Bert had difficulty putting all the information together. Betty told him that Jean had been seeing an American soldier and had got in the family way.

He wanted to know, "How could she get pregnant just seeing him?"

Betty laughed at him. "When I say seeing, I don't mean looking. I mean you-know-what. Now she's up the duff. The problem is he can't marry her. He's engaged to a girl back in California. Jean's heartbroken."

They were outside the school gates. Betty had come by to walk home with him as planned. If there was no suspicious-looking vehicle, they would go up to the bakery. A whole week had gone by, and although Donald's photo was still stuck on lamp posts and in shop windows, it looked as though the door-to-door search in their street had ended.

"What will she do?" he asked.

"Who?"

"Jean. How can she go to work and look after a baby by herself?"

"There's no way she can keep it. She'll have it adopted out. That's why she's so upset."

Bert wondered why Betty knew so much, but of course, that would be Aunty Vi. She and Betty always had their heads together. He rattled a piece of stick along a corrugated-iron fence. The noise was very satisfying. Betty probably knew more about babies and that sort of stuff than he did. He broke the stick in half and wished he had had a brother. Sisters were so complicated.

"G'day Bert!" It was Reggie on the other side of the road, crossing over to see Betty. Reggie always did that. "How are you, Betty Grable?" He always did that, too, calling her after the film star.

"Go home, Reggie," Betty said in a weary voice.

"Want to go to the flicks with me?" Reggie teased.

She didn't answer, and Bert scowled. "Buzz off, Reg!"

But Reggie didn't go. He fell into step behind her, chanting, "Betty Grable's got good legs, look like a couple of wooden pegs. Betty Grable's got good tits, look like a couple of battleships."

Betty's answer to that was to whirl around and swipe Reggie across the side of his head. "Clear off, or I'll give you a good bashing!" she said.

"Ow!" He held the side of his head. "You're a witch! You're a stinking crabby witch!"

"You want another one?" Betty raised her hand.

Reggie ran back across the road, and once he was on the other side he yelled a few choice swear words and put his thumb to his nose.

Betty laughed.

"Reggie goes too far," muttered Bert. "He didn't mean it."

Betty didn't seem too bothered. She changed the subject. "I hope you haven't started collecting lunches again."

"No," he said. "Not since those MPs have been snooping around."

She draped an arm over Bert's shoulders. "There's a notice at high school. It's in the assembly hall. Got his picture on it like he's some film star."

"Our school, too."

They were silent for a while, and Bert was thinking danger, danger. It was like those cowboy movies where a bandit's picture, offering a hundred dollars reward, was posted on a wall. Once people knew the face, there was no way of being invisible.

They reached their road and started the climb up the hill. Grey cloud was closing down the day and it would be a cold night. Bert had an extra eiderdown on his stretcher bed, and it made him wonder how Donald was keeping warm. Betty had taken him two old grey blankets from the top of her wardrobe, but that wasn't enough in midwinter.

"Thank goodness for Aunty Vi," said Betty. "Last night she gave me a whole luncheon sausage, a loaf of bread and a packet of Chesdale cheese."

Bert smiled. "For the stray dog?"

"Of course. For the stray dog."

When they reached their house, Betty went in, unloaded her school books and came out again with a heavy case. Bert waited outside the fence. There wasn't much in his school bag – his extra sandwiches, a couple of torch batteries, and a torch that Alwyn had given him in exchange for a bundle of comics.

When they reached the Geronimo bakehouse, they walked carefully, staying close to the building so they wouldn't leave tracks in the grass or stumble into the booby traps.

The trapdoor was at the side but couldn't be seen from the road, or anywhere else for that matter. Pine trees and wild scrub ringed the property. Not a soul in sight.

Donald was extra pleased to see them, and he liked Bert's torch. "Gee! You got extra batteries, too. That's corker! The candles are okay but sometimes I need extra light." He switched on the torch and

Bert saw that his face and hands were clean and his hair tidy. Some towels and a khaki shirt were hanging from the hooks above the bench. Donald followed Bert's gaze. "They take ages to dry in here."

Betty put her case on the bench and opened it. "Look!"

He came over and shone the torch her way. "Oh, boy! That's a whole luncheon sausage! Bread! Cheese! I never got fed like this, not even in the army." He put his hand on Betty's shoulder. "Are you staying? Aw, come on! Let's have a feast."

Betty laughed. "No, we have to get back. Mum'll be waiting."

Donald didn't take his hand off her shoulder and she didn't move away.

He said, "Can't you stay just a little while? Crikey, I've been sitting here all day thinking—" He stopped and looked at Bert. "You know something? I've had a go at cleaning the place up for you. Your bomb shelter!" He moved away from Betty and played the torch beam around the big room.

"I've scrubbed the benches, scraped the rust off the stoves. Looks good, doesn't it? Gives me something to do. I got to do something or I'll end up in the loony bin. I sometimes talk to myself. Waste of time that, telling yourself things you already know." He laughed.

"It looks beaut," Bert said. "Even Mum would

think it was clean. When the invasion comes, they'll come here like it's their home—" He glanced at Donald. "But you won't be here then. You'll be on that sheep farm."

Betty fidgeted. "Sorry. We really have to go."

Donald's smile vanished. "Right now at this moment?"

"That's the truth," said Betty. "But I'll be back."

"Again tonight? You promise?"

"What do you think?" said Betty, giving him one of her sly smiles.

Bert stepped forward. "Too right! We'll be back. We have to go now."

On the way down the hill, Bert asked Betty why she had promised to go back. "You know we can't."

"Not you! But I can." She pressed her fingers against her lips and then waved them at him. "You wait and see."

That evening, after the blackout siren had sounded, Betty put on her coat and hat. She waved a postcard. "Won't be long," she said. "I've just written a note to Uncle Mack, and I'm going down to the mailbox. Is there anything I can get anyone?"

Dad looked at her. "Leave it. I'll take it to the Post Office in the morning."

"I want it to go in the mail tonight," Betty said.

Dad shook his head and grunted, his way of saying there was no point arguing with Betty.

"I don't need anything, thanks, dear," said Mum. "Be careful."

Betty gave Bert a meaningful smile and ran out, her coat flapping at her back.

CHAPTER THIRTEEN

They had avoided taking Meg to the Geronimo bakehouse, afraid of what she might say in one of her careless moments. Now she was insisting that she wanted to see the soldier, and Betty said, "Okay, we'll all go."

Bert thought that was fair since Meg had held fast to her promise not to tell.

"We're taking Meg to the playground," he told Mum.

They had to go there first to make it true, but after a quick slide and a couple of pushes on the swing, they were on their way to the bakery, Meg clutching an early daffodil she had picked through someone's fence.

Donald was pleased with the flower and he put it in a jar of water on the big bench. "My nanna used to grow daffodils," he said.

"Your nanna will be sad for you." Meg's eyes were round with concern.

"No. My nanna died three years ago."

That was when he told them that his mother had not been able to look after him and he had lived with his grandmother until he was fifteen.

Bert immediately thought of Jean having to adopt out her baby, and he guessed Betty was making the same connections. What would happen to Jean? he wondered. What would happen to the baby? Would it go into an orphanage?

They were sitting on the concrete floor between the old stoves and the benches. It was clean now, scrubbed, and Donald had spread a square of fabric on it, could have been a rug or a tablecloth, another of the things he had nicked. He put his plate on it, and Betty unpacked the food they had brought: more bread, a couple of stale sausage rolls, two ripe pears, and some of Aunty Vi's chocolate bars. Donald broke one of the bars into four and they all had a piece.

"What did you do when you were fifteen?" Meg asked.

"Nanna got ill and had to go to hospital. I got a job on a poultry farm. It was a good job. I like animals. I always wanted to work on a farm." The glow of the candle made moving points of light in his dark eyes. "I'd still be there but conscription came along."

"His grandmother died when he was sixteen," Betty explained, and Bert realised that she already knew the story of Donald's life. He wondered why she hadn't told him about it.

"I wasn't much good in the army," Donald said. "It suits some blokes, but I never got it right. They said I lacked moral fibre. We did a route march over the Rimutaka hill. I got blisters. The skin was hanging off my feet. I couldn't walk. The next day the sergeant took me behind the latrines and punched the hell out of me. Not in the face. Chest and stomach. I thought I was going to die. But that's the way things are. The other blokes didn't seem to mind being pushed around."

Meg's eyes were wide with shock and she had her hand over her mouth.

"It wasn't all bad," he said. "Some of the chaps were really nice. But they thought I was soft. They called me Petal." He smiled. "I never did harden up. Then we learned we were being shipped to the Pacific to fight the Japanese. I knew, absolutely knew I wouldn't last. I – I couldn't kill anybody – not even a chicken."

Bert felt sorry for the poor coot. Yes, he was a bit soft and he would probably have got himself wiped out in the first action. But it was now looking hopeful that they could get him to his uncle's place. Betty was holding the two pounds from Aunty Vi, and soon they would be able to buy him clothes and maybe a razor and put him on a ferry to the South Island.

"What about your uncle?" he said. "Can you trust him?"

"You bet." Donald smiled. "He knew conscription was coming and he wrote to me. Wanted me to be with him on this big sheep station – miles and miles of hills in the middle of nowhere, he said. But I quite liked the poultry farm. Two thousand white chooks, laying all those eggs. You know eggs are warm when they're laid? They're soft, too. The shell hardens as it gets to the air. Well, I thought I'd miss the draft. My boss told me that – reckoned the army wouldn't take me because I've got flat feet. Cripes, was he wrong! They don't care what kind of feet we got." He picked up a sausage roll and stuffed it all into his mouth, chewed and chewed, swallowed, and wiped his mouth with the back of his hand. "You kids have been bloody marvellous," he said, and he gently poked Bert and then Meg.

It was only after they left that Bert realised he hadn't included Betty. Maybe that was because Betty wasn't exactly a kid. Petal, he thought. His nickname was Petal. Had Betty known that?

Late that night, he was wakened by his father, standing in the doorway of the sun-porch with a torch. He blinked and rubbed his eyes. With the light in his face, he didn't know it was Dad until he spoke. "Are you awake?"

"Yeah."

"Do you know where your sister is?"

"What?"

"Betty! Do you know where she is?"

Bert's mind was only half awake, but it was saying to him, caution, caution. "Isn't she in bed?"

"No. Her bed is empty. Meg had a nightmare and your mother went in. The other bed had two pillows in it to look like a sleeping body."

Bert didn't know what to say. He'd told Betty she'd get caught, but she'd laughed and said that Meg slept like a log and there was no danger.

Now, it seemed that everyone was up, Mum, Aunty Vi in her pink dressing gown, Meg, looking sleepy and confused.

Mum put her arm around Meg and said to Bert, "She was crying about someone being punched in the stomach. Is that one of your stories?"

"No." He hesitated. "It might have been."

"You should know better," Mum said. "Where's Betty?"

"I don't know."

Aunty Vi said, "She probably went for a walk."

"A walk?" said Dad. "At this time of night?"

"Sure," said Aunty Vi. "We often go on a night walk together. Maybe she looked in and saw I was asleep, so off she went on her own."

Bert didn't dare look at Aunty Vi, but he wanted to. He wanted to tell her that she was a star and she should get a prize for best aunty.

"I'm going out to look for her!" Dad looked angry, but frightened, too. He went into the bedroom to get dressed.

Mum said to Aunty Vi, "Why on earth would you take a teenage girl out for a walk in the middle of the night? Dick's right, Vi. You lack a sense of responsibility."

Aunty Vi shrugged. "Oh come off it, honey bun. You know me. I never did the ordinary."

"Don't call me honey bun," said Mum. "I don't need any of your Americanisms in this house, thank you very much."

"Oh, hot diggity!" Aunty Vi laughed and nudged her sister with her elbow.

Bert wanted to laugh and say, Good for you, Aunty Vi, but he didn't dare.

Bert was wild with Betty for creating this problem. You are so selfish, he would tell her. You say and do what you like without a thought for anyone else. What do you think you are playing at?

Dad came out of the bedroom, dressed in his old clothes with a heavy coat, but before he got near the door it opened and in came Betty. She was in her Sunday dress with her raincoat on top. Her eyes went still for a moment as she took in the situation, then she said, "Hello! Everyone's up early."

"Where the blazes have you been!" said Dad.

"Out for a walk."

"At this time of night? On your own?" said Mum.

Aunty Vi interrupted. "I told you. I usually go with her."

Betty was quick. She caught that ball on the full. She turned to Aunty Vi. "Sorry, you were sound asleep."

Bert saw his father's mouth go thin, and the muscles around his jaw tighten in anger. Then Dad looked at Aunty Vi, at Betty, and said, "Go to bed. We'll talk about this in the morning."

CHAPTER FOURTEEN

Bert thought it was lousy to be kept from information by a gang of women. There was a weight of female whispers in the house; even Mum was a part of it. No one told him what was happening to Jean, who hadn't been back to the house since that night. If he asked Betty questions, she fobbed him off with non-answers or downright lies. Betty was good at lying. She thought she had a right to deceive him because he was her young brother. He knew that she had been to see Donald in the night, but she insisted it was just a walk down the road. "Why would I go to see him? We'd already taken him supplies."

Dad was grumpy, though not with Betty. He was taking it out on Aunty Vi. Although he'd said they would talk about it in the morning, all he offered at the breakfast table was a huge, punishing silence. The one who wasn't at all worried was Aunty Vi. She chatted on and on, about a woman at work who had long hair and used to pluck out a hair to darn her silk stockings. Mum joined in and there was more talk about rationing and stockings until Dad said "Hush!" and they all had to be quiet for the news.

This is the BBC London calling …

There was nothing about the Japanese invasion of the South Pacific. It was all about the battles in Russia and Germany. British bombers had bombed the city of Cologne. Hundreds of people had died and thousands were wounded.

"Oh dear Lord!" Mum's hands were clasped at her chest. "How terrible!"

Bert was wondering if Uncle Mack's plane had been doing the bombing. He desperately wanted to think it was. That would show those Huns a thing or two.

Then he thought of Donald shut up in the bakehouse. Being killed by the enemy was one thing. Being shot by your own side was entirely different.

Dad turned to Mum. "If you think that's terrible, how about this? RAAF planes have spotted the place where the Jerries are making long-range rocket bombs. Long-range! That means they'll be able to fire them right over the Channel."

Mum shuddered, and leaned across the table to collect their empty plates.

Then Aunty Vi said, "Is it likely Mack would have been in that bombing raid?" She looked worried, and Bert wanted to tell her he probably was, and the war was a lot bigger than mending a silk stocking. He didn't even know if it was right for Aunty Vi to be happy when her husband was flying with a load of bombs on serious missions. Did she know how many pilots died? Maybe she should read the newspapers instead of going out to dances.

None of them knew that Uncle Mack had not been on the Cologne raid. It was a while before they got the cablegram. He had smashed his right leg, not in a plane but in a car. He and two other pilots had been at a village pub and, on the way back to base, had gone off the road. The car had rolled, killing the driver and pinning Mack by the leg. The other passenger had minor injuries, but Mack's was more serious. He was in hospital. His lower leg could not be saved.

CHAPTER
FIFTEEN

All the fun went out of Aunty Vi when she got the news, and she cried streaks of tears. "He won't be able to play tennis!" she said. "He loved tennis!"

Bert thought that was an odd thing to say, but at times Aunty Vi was odd.

Mum stroked her arm. "It could have been worse, dear. Look at it this way. They'll send him home."

Aunty Vi's wet eyes brightened. "Do you think so?"

"Oh yes. He'll have a wooden leg fitted so he'll be able to walk nearly as well as before, and that's the war over for him. You'll have him back! Would you like another cup of tea?"

A while later, all the hospital details came from Uncle Mack, slanted black writing in a blue aerogramme. Rotten luck, he wrote, terrible to lose his mate Jock in such an ungallant way, flying fifteen missions and then turning turtle in a car. Car was a total write-off. But he was all right, amputation healing nicely, only it was funny that the missing part of his leg hurt as though it was still there. He'd get an artificial limb made to order, and be back at the base soon, no flying, a ground job, probably radio, though he wouldn't mind helping the maintenance crew. Cheerio, Sport, and don't worry about me. I'll soon be up and at them again. Lots of love, Mack.

"So he's not coming home," said Aunty Vi.

"They need him!" Mum hugged her sister. "It just goes to show how valuable he is. They can't run the place without him."

Aunty Vi was disappointed, but Bert understood why Uncle Mack was staying. Men had to do their duty. Well, most men. Women didn't understand how important that was.

If men didn't go out and fight to protect their country, the world would be a huge mess. Civilisation would disappear.

Later, Aunty Vi saw Betty and Bert in the kitchen. She put an arm around each, and ushered them into Bert's sun-porch where they would not be heard. "How is your stray dog?" she asked.

"Good," said Betty.

"Is he still sick?"

"No, he's much better."

Bert said, "His cough has gone."

Aunty Vi squeezed her arms around them so that their heads were almost touching hers. "It's time to find that home for him."

"That's what we decided," said Bert. "We're going to buy some clothes and get him on the—"

"Stop!" She took her arms away and waved her hands in front of her, as though to clear the air. "I don't want to know. It's a stray dog! Remember?"

Bert felt embarrassed. He knew the rules, but he had done a Meg in blurting out the forbidden. "Sorry," he murmured.

Aunty Vi smoothed back her hair. She still looked as though all the laughter had been drained out of her. "He needs to disappear," she said, and she walked away.

Bert looked at Betty. "Do you think it's safe now?"

"It's nearly a month," she said. "They're not looking for him. They probably think he's miles away."

Bert knew that the pictures pasted on lamp posts and public buildings had peeled off in the rain, and the 'Have you see this man?' sign in the corridor at his school had disappeared. There was still a photo of Donald in the milkshake bar where New Zealand soldiers gathered to play the jukeboxes. It was stuck inside the window, looking out into the street. But that was only one place.

After school, the misty drizzle hardened to steady rain, and Bert needed his oilskin coat with the hood turned up to walk to the Geronimo bakehouse. Under the coat he clutched the usual sandwiches and some cold Yorkshire pudding from last night's meal. The sky was grey and heavy, clouds resting on tall trees, and there was mist lying in the hollows. By the time he got to the trapdoor, water was running off his coat. With one arm against his chest to hold the food, he jumped down and pulled the trapdoor shut behind him. In the darkness of the coal place, he shook himself before moving towards the big room. A single candle glowed on the bench, and drops of water fell through holes in the roof, splashing on the floor.

Donald came out of the side room. He smiled at Bert, then looked past him.

"Not today," Bert said. "It's her turn with Meg."

"I wasn't expecting Betty," Donald said quickly.

Bert thought that, unlike his sister, the soldier was a poor liar. He unbuttoned his oilskin. "I've got the usual rations."

"Wet out there, isn't it?" said Donald, taking the wet coat.

Bert looked hard and saw that Donald's hair was damp. "Have you been outside?"

"Nowhere near the road. I'm careful. And no one's looking for me in the rain. It's cold, but gee, do you know how good it feels to be out in the air with rain falling from the sky? I needed that!"

"You got rain falling in here," said Bert, pointing to the leaking roof. "Why risk getting caught?"

"I really am careful — very, very careful. Bert, I need to see daylight and feel growing things. Just for a few minutes. Crikey, this place is like a dungeon. Solitary confinement!" Then he added quickly. "Except for you, of course. So it's not really solitary. Is anyone looking for me? What have you heard?"

"Nothing." Bert shook his head. "No patrols. We think you should make a move. Has Betty told you the plan? Tomorrow we're going to a second-hand shop to get you an outfit, some strides, shirt, pullover. You can't wear that girl's Fair Isle jersey. It'll attract attention. Like you've pinched it off someone's clothes line. Some kind of jacket, maybe, one that looks like a school blazer. No hat. It'll make you look too old. You're sixteen, remember! Not nineteen. You'll have to think of a new name for yourself."

"I already have," said Donald. "I'll be David Carter."

"Mistake!" said Bert. "David Carter, Donald Curtis, you're using the same initials. Better think again."

"Thanks. I will. What happens then?"

"You'll get a ticket for the overnight ferry to Christchurch, and enough money for buses the rest of the way. We've talked about it, and it should work. If anyone asks you where you're going, tell them Queenstown, Invercargill – anywhere but the place where your uncle lives. We'll get you a map. Remind us about that. At the end of the journey you might have to do a bit of walking, but at least you'll be free."

When Donald smiled fully, he showed all his front teeth. They were a bit uneven, like fence palings come loose. "Thank you, thank you! You've been bloody marvellous and I'll never forget it. I told you I'll pay you back. Honest to God, I will. I'll send back every penny."

"No!" Bert stepped back. "You mustn't do that! Don't do anything that can be traced back to our family." Then he said slowly, emphasising each word. "Don't write any letters – to any of us! It could put us in prison!"

The smile vanished and Donald's face went blank. "Really?"

"Too right! No postcards! No letters! Nothing!"

Now the look was one of misery.

"I'd better be going," Bert said.

Donald helped him into his wet coat. "Is it Betty's turn tomorrow?" he asked in a small boy's voice.

"Could be," said Bert. "But then, it might be me."

CHAPTER SIXTEEN

When Bert was on Geronimo bakehouse duty, he left school promptly and had at least half an hour free before Mum started looking at the clock. But Betty was changing the system. Ever since she'd been caught, she'd cut out those stupid night walks and was claiming more afternoons with Donald. The reason was now obvious. She had a crush on him. Nearly every time she returned, she was either smiling or singing, or both. It was so annoying to see her making a fool of herself, and it was a jolly good thing Donald would be out of their lives soon.

He was pleased, though, that no one had suspected – only Aunty Vi, and she was on their side. The alarm about the local burglar had faded, Mum probably wouldn't want her towels back now anyway, and other things had filled family conversations. The war was always there, like a big hungry ghost that poured itself out of the radio to haunt the house. Then there was the thing about Jean, and now all the talk was around poor Uncle Mack losing some of his leg. At least, thought Bert, Dad had been nicer to Aunty Vi since that accident. He told her about a man he knew who played golf with a wooden leg. Aunt Vi had smiled. "Really? I thought he'd use a golf club." Dad actually laughed.

For breakfast Mum made scrambled egg with egg powder, never as good as real eggs, but she put fried onions with it and it was okay, a change from porridge. Bert had a big helping and scooped half of it into a jar when no one was looking. Today he and Betty needed to go into the city to the second-hand shop, which had heaps and heaps of clothes. Bert thought they needed to tell Mum they were getting a tram into town after school, and Betty said, "I'll fix it." But it was Aunty Vi she talked to, and in front of their parents, Aunty Vi said, "How about you two coming into Woolworths today to see Jean and me? We've got a little something tucked away for you."

"Jean?" Bert was surprised. He though Aunty Vi's friend had gone away to have a baby.

Betty gave him a 'Shut up!' look and he closed his mouth, as Aunty Vi put four pennies on the table for their tram fares. But when they were ready to leave for school, he asked Betty about Jean.

"Of course Jean's still working," said Betty. "She'll stay until she starts showing."

"Showing what?"

"Don't you know anything about babies?"

He was silent. Although Dad had told him that babies came to married people, he hadn't said anything that could explain Jean's situation.

'I've got to go." Betty picked up her case. "Look, I'll tell you about Jean later, okay?"

"Yeah," he said, although he was hoping she'd forget. Ignorance was embarrassing, but so, he thought, was knowing. Whatever had happened to Jean had also happened between Bert's parents, and he wasn't sure he was ready to think about it.

That morning, school was different. There was a general assembly and a minute's silence for the husband of Mrs Holt who taught Standard Three. Lieutenant Holt had died when his ship was torpedoed in the North Sea. Mrs Holt was not at school, and the headmaster, Mr Grimshaw, took her class. Bert stood with the others, arms at his side, thinking that Uncle Mack was lucky having just one bit of him dead. He thought of Mrs Holt. She hadn't taught him, but she looked a nice lady, had a happy face. She wouldn't be happy now. A minute was a long time. The silence crashed around them like breaking waves, and then it was over. Music was played over the loudspeakers and they marched into class, left, right, left, right.

Bert thought it was like one of those military funeral marches you saw on newsreels.

It was something to tell Betty. There had been a buzz of talk all day at school, and by the time he met Betty at the tram stop he felt so close to Mrs Holt and her husband that his death was big news. It wasn't big news for Betty, though. She wanted to talk about clothes for Donald. Blast Donald! The good thing was she forgot she was going to tell him about babies.

At Woolworths, Jean, who was usually at the crockery counter, came over to Aunty Vi at confectionary to say hello to them. As far as Bert could see, Jean didn't look any different from normal. Her yellow hair was in a roll around her face and she had bright red lipstick, same as always.

Aunty Vi gave them a bag with four raspberry buns she'd bought at the cake shop.

Jean handed them a packet of liquorice straps. "Don't eat them all at once, or you'll be in trouble," she said with a giggle.

Bert hadn't seen Jean since all that crying in their living room, and her laughter brought relief. It cancelled the shadow of worry that lay over his thoughts about her. For some reason he had been sure she'd still be bawling her eyes out.

They didn't waste too much time at Woolworths. They walked quickly three streets to the second-hand store. As they crossed a road, a young American soldier called to Betty, "Hi, Babe! How ya doing?"

Betty turned, smiled and waved. "Hello."

"You should have ignored him," Bert growled.

She gave him a pitying look. "Gee, Bert, you sound just like Dad at times."

The second-hand store had everything from old bicycles to chinaware to gramophone records, but about half the space had racks and shelves of clothes. With so much interesting stuff, Bert left the clothes shopping to Betty. She'd get what she wanted, anyway. He saw an old bike with flat tyres for five shillings, but he already had a bike he hardly ever rode because their hill was too steep. Tools! A good box plane, for Dad's shed, only sixpence! A china dog that Mum would like, just a small chip out of its ear – tuppence!

Then he thought, stray dog, and looked at the clothing area, where Betty was searching through shirts on hangers. He walked across the floor. When the Donald thing was over, he'd come back here with his pocket money. The place was full of bargains.

Betty had already picked out a blue shirt and a navy blue knitted jersey. "These will look good together."

"How do you know they'll fit?" he asked.

She shrugged. "If they don't, I'll bring them back and change them." She wrinkled her nose. "Heck, this place stinks. Sweat! Old shoes!"

The shop did have a distinctive smell, but Bert thought it was kind of friendly, like being in a crowded tram. "What about shoes?" he said. "You don't know his size."

"Yes, I do – elevens." She took from the rack a dark grey flannel blazer, shiny with wear. "What do you think of this?"

"It looks like a high school jacket," he said.

"Good," she said, and draped it over her arm.

They got the whole lot for less than three shillings. Some of it, they packed in Betty's school case. The rest went into two brown paper bags. As they left the shop, Betty said, "I'll have time to take it up to him this afternoon."

He corrected her. "We'll take it up."

"No. You will go home. I'll go straight there, and you can tell Mum I'm coming on a later tram."

"Why can't I come? It was my money, too."

"Don't argue, Bert. We can't both be late. Give me those raspberry buns. He'll think all his Christmases have come at once."

On the way home in the tram, he was quiet, his mind creating something to say to Mum that wasn't exactly a lie. He wasn't Betty. She could tell a whopper without blinking once. He leaned across and looked at the watch Mum and Dad had given her for her fifteenth birthday. Twenty-five minutes past four. Yes, she'd have time to go up the hill to the Geronimo bakehouse and be home soon after five. But he was still annoyed at being left out, like a football kicked into touch.

He didn't need to excuse her to Mum. His mother wasn't home, and neither was Meg. The house was empty, silent, the afternoon sun a puddle on the kitchen lino. It was a while before he found his mother's note beside the toaster on the kitchen table. *Meg's got earache again. I'm taking her to the doctor. When you get home, put on the potatoes and get a cabbage from the garden. Love, Mum.*

Bert took out a knife and wondered which should come first, cabbage or potatoes, and then decided neither. His mind tripped up on a thought about Mrs Holt. Her husband was either floating dead in the North Sea or eaten by sharks, and here he was concerned about cabbages and potatoes. How dumb was that? He put down the knife and stared at the wall. Did sharks eat uniforms? Or just the bodies inside? No, he shouldn't be thinking horrible things about Lieutenant Holt.

He hit his head with the flat of his hand. Cabbages, cabbages! Uniforms! Betty had chosen all Donald's clothes. Everything. Jacket, shirt, trousers, shoes. This was Betty taking over again! How could she be so sure of the size? If they were the wrong fit, Donald would look as though he'd stolen stuff off clothes lines, and any soldiers on the ferry would notice the man in the odd outfit, take a closer look, and think, Well, what do you know, it's the deserter chap.

Then came the other thought. If they were the right size, how did she know? The soldier could have told her. Maybe she looked at the size of his uniform, or she took Mum's tape measure and put it against him, up and down and around.

Bert threw the knife across the bench and it landed on the floor.

He looked again at the clock. It was early. He could still get up there and be back again in time to put on the vegetables. Betty wasn't the boss of the world.

Bert picked up the knife and put it back in the drawer.

Aunty Vi had given them each a one-pound note. Their birthday money, she said. And Betty had taken his money as well as her own. Not that he minded. But the trapdoor to the Geronimo bakehouse was his find, the bomb shelter was his idea, so why had she put herself in charge, doing the buying, making all the rules about Donald? This business of writing to him! What was that about? A schoolgirl and a deserter sending letters to each other!

He ran all the way up the steep slope from his house to the old brick building, and lifted the trapdoor enough to roll in and drop down. Bert landed on his hands and knees in damp coal dust. He stood and brushed off the gritty bits before checking that the trapdoor was properly shut behind him. As always there was a moment of complete darkness and then his eyes adjusted to a small glow of light in the big room of the bakehouse. A candle was burning in a jar on the bench, a small halo of brightness around it. He saw the brown paper bags on the floor, the jacket, the shoes spread, one upside down with the light glinting on heel and toe plates. There was also a plate further away, with two raspberry buns and some crumbs on it. Where were they?

Bert peered into the side room and saw only darkness, but there was a small movement, and a sound like the catch of a breath, and he made out a figure standing near the wall. No, two figures standing. She had her arms around him, and he had his arms around her. Their heads were together.

They were kissing.

CHAPTER SEVENTEEN

She was furious. All the way down the hill she shouted at him.

"Spying on me, you sneaky little rat! Who do you think you are? It would serve you right if I never spoke to you again in your entire miserable life!"

"I saw you," he muttered.

"Saw what? Nothing! We haven't done anything wrong. I'm not stupid like Jean! We were just saying goodbye. You've got an evil little mind!"

He kicked a pebble. "He's got two more days there. How come it's goodbye?"

"You don't know what you're talking about, so keep your mouth shut or I'll shut it for you!" Her eyes were narrow and as hard as stone. "I totally forbid you to go near him again. Is that clear?"

"You can't stop me."

"Oh yes I can! For your information, Donald doesn't want to see you."

"He does! He said so!"

"Not now, he doesn't." She lowered her voice as they neared the house.

"Not after you told him a pack of lies."

"What lies?"

She stopped, her hand on the gate latch. "The letter writing! You said if he wrote a letter to me, I would go to prison. You did, didn't you? What were you playing at?" So that was what had made her mad!

"It wasn't exactly those words," he said. "I was worried he'd get caught."

"Don't lie!" she hissed.

He thought she was a fine one to talk about lying, and would have told her so, but she was through the gate, slamming it behind her. "You're not being fair!" he shouted. The back door also slammed. He took a deep breath and opened the gate, trudged up the path and followed her, through the hall and into her room. He tried to explain. "The reason I said it was because there is a real danger—"

Wham! The door shut in his face, almost hitting his nose. He went back to the kitchen and pulled down the blackout blinds before switching on the light. You could never argue with Betty. But give her time and she'd get over it. He'd better peel those potatoes for Mum, and get a cabbage from the garden.

The spuds were cooked when Mum came in with Meg, who had cotton wool in one ear and a tear-streaked face. Mum glanced at the stove. "Thank you, dear. There was a big crowd in the surgery, and then we had to wait for a prescription. Otitis media. She had pus coming out of her ear. Two bottles of drops – ear and nose. Have you cooked the cabbage? Where is Betty?"

Betty didn't come out of the bedroom. Aunty Vi came home, then Dad, and by then it was time to black out all the windows in the house and light the fire in the living room. There was no meat tonight, so it was baked beans with potatoes and cabbage and thick slices of toast. Betty came when she was called, and she talked to everyone except Bert. She actually looked as though she was in a good mood, laughing, telling them about a girl in her class who had wagged school to go to the pictures and had sat next to her mother, not seeing her in the dark. But when she said the last words about seeing in the dark, she turned dead cold eyes on Bert, who quickly looked away.

He saw them. He did. They were kissing. It looked more like hello than goodbye, like they were trying to eat each other, their faces squashed together.

Why was she blaming him? None of it was his fault.

"How's your teacher?" Dad asked. "The one whose husband drowned?"

"That wasn't my teacher. It was Mrs Holt in Standard Three," he said. "She's still away. Mr Grimshaw is teaching her class."

Dad nodded. "It would be a nice thing to write a letter of sympathy, don't you think?"

"We had a minute of silence in assembly."

"I mean you," Dad said. "You could write her a letter. It would be a boy's contribution to the war effort."

"I suppose so." Bert looked around the table and noticed that no one was eating their cabbage. It looked grey and slimy. He had boiled it too long. He steered the talk away from a letter to Mrs Holt. "Sorry about the cabbage. I overcooked it."

Aunty Vi gave him one of her full-face smiles. "All the best chefs learn from their mistakes. It's fine, kiddo."

He smiled back. "No it's not." He paused, then deliberately added. "Even a stray dog wouldn't eat it."

Aunty Vi blinked, but Betty's face didn't change. He hoped she would smile. Instead, she looked right through him as though she was seeing his empty chair. She was still mad at him. Never mind. She'd cool down.

When the meal was over and the table cleared, Bert pulled out a blank page from his essay book, and wrote the letter.

Dear Mrs Holt,

I am writing this to tell you how sorry I am about Mr Holt. (He crossed out Mr Holt and looked at Mum, who was wiping down the bench. "How do you spell Lieutenant?" She told him and he continued.) *All our school feels very sorry for you. We had a minute's silence. Mr Grimshaw is teaching your class in Standard Three.* He chewed the end of his pencil.

"Is this all right?" he asked Mum.

The dishcloth still in her hands, she looked over his shoulder. "You might like to add something personal."

"Like what?"

"A few words about how you feel," Mum said.

He sat for a while, then wrote, *If my dad died in the war I would be very sad and angry. I would go and bom the submarine that fired the torpedo.*

Mum pointed. "You left out the b in bomb."

"No, I didn't."

"Yes dear. There! It begins and ends with b."

He looked again. She was right. "Oh yeah. I did. B for Betty."

"B for Bertie," said Mum. She gave him a mother look. "What are you two fighting about?"

"Nothing."

"If it's nothing, why are you glaring at each other?"

"It's not me, it's her." He stopped, unable to say more.

Mum sighed. "I'll get you an envelope and Dad can take it in the morning."

"I don't know where Mrs Holt lives," he said, glad that the subject had changed. "All the teachers know her address. I'll take the letter to school tomorrow and leave it in the staffroom. Thanks, Mum."

His mother gave him a quick sideways hug. "Good boy. Don't forget to say goodnight to Betty."

CHAPTER EIGHTEEN

He did say goodnight to Betty, but she ignored him. The next morning, however, she waited for him outside the gate, which usually meant she wanted to walk with him down the hill. That was good. He'd be able to explain what he meant about not getting letters from Donald. It's risky, he'd tell her. It could affect everyone, even Mum and Dad. It was against the law to help a deserter, and Donald was a thief as well. He had taken things from their neighbours. Mum and Dad would get the blame because it was their kids who had broken the law.

But Betty didn't want to hear any of it. As he closed the gate, she said in a low voice, "This is a reminder. You don't go to see him after school today. That's definite."

They set off down the hill. "I was only trying to protect you," he said. "I was thinking of our family!

Honest! What happens if Mum finds his letters?"

"She won't. He'll send them to me care of a girl at school – and I'm not telling you who. Stay away from the bakehouse! You can go there after he's gone. I'm getting the ferry ticket today."

"What time's he going?" He glanced at her, but she was looking straight ahead and her face was hard. "Tomorrow morning?" he said. "Afternoon?"

She didn't answer, and her coldness was a freezing pain inside his head, like eating ice cream too fast.

At last he said it. "I – I know you like him. He likes you, too. Doesn't he?"

Even that did not make her talk. But halfway down the hill, she said, "Do you know what an understanding is?"

"Huh? Understanding what?"

"Donald's explained it. He and I have an understanding. It's like a promise. We are going to write to each other every week, and when the war is over we're getting married." She looked at him through narrowed eyes. "If you say anything to anyone, I'll not only deny it, I'll make you wish you'd never been born. Is that clear, you little turd?" Then she stepped ahead quickly and walked in front of him to the tram stop.

He didn't try to catch up.

The sky was blue above the sea, but there was no promise of warmth. The morning sun made winter-black shadows across the pavement, and in those shadows were patches of frost. The word *married* stuck in his head, sounding over and over, in her voice. She couldn't get married, he argued. She was Betty. She was fifteen. She didn't really mean it. She was just saying it to make him mad. All the boys chased after her. Once Donald went to his uncle's farm, she'd have a crush on someone else.

But at the same time, he knew it wasn't true. When Betty got her teeth into something, she didn't let go. "No use arguing with Betty," their father always said. Like that business of Betty taking a library book to church. Dad argued and threatened but she still did it, and in the end Dad gave up and pretended Betty wasn't reading all through the sermon.

He had a miserable day at school. His head ached, his stomach hurt, and he got told off by Mrs Alsop because he couldn't recite the eight times table, which he actually knew by heart. At morning break he took Mrs Holt's letter to the staffroom and was surprised to see a heap of letters in a basket that had her name on it. A lot of kids had been writing. He thought at first he had wasted his time, but then decided it was okay. Reading a basket full of letters would give Mrs Holt something to do. He wished that he had something to do to help take away his own pain.

After school, Alwyn and Tim wanted him to play splash tag, a game they had invented. It involved throwing a wet ball of paper and usually it was fun. But today his head still hurt and he walked back through the shopping centre, pausing at the milkshake bar to look at the photo of Donald in the window.

It was a stupid photo. Private Curtis was smiling as though military training was a game, and he expected to have fun. That was a big lie. Everything was a lie! Bert's head pounded something awful. Like there were drops of blood in his brain, hard as red bullets bouncing against his skull and exploding. Lie, lie, lie.

At the edge of the pavement, a New Zealand Army truck with a cover over the tray had its motor running, fumes and steam forming a cloud behind the exhaust pipe. There was a soldier sitting behind the wheel, smoking a cigarette and flicking ash out the window. He looked as though he was bored with waiting.

Inside the milkshake bar, four soldiers pushed their chairs back, stood and said something to the waitress, who wore a pink dress. They were laughing. When they came out the door, she called after them, "You know your ABC, boys – always be careful." It wasn't funny, but they acted as though it was. One of them said to the others, "I wouldn't mind putting my shoes under her bed," and then the driver of the truck sounded the horn to make them hurry up. They didn't go faster. They jostled each other with their elbows and their boots scuffed the pavement. One after the other they went past Bert, and the first soldier put his foot on the running-board of the truck. He was about to climb into the back when Bert ran forward. "Hey!" he shouted, and the sound was a bomb going off in his head.

They looked at him, surprised.

"I've seen the deserter!" he yelled. "The one in the photograph."

The man took his foot off the running-board. "Who?"

"Him!" He pointed to the picture in the window.

"He means Curtis," said one of the others, and suddenly the laughter was gone. The soldiers went as still as statues and looked at him with sharp eyes, as though this was a trick, a kid wasting their time. "You've seen him?"

He nodded.

They moved in closer and he could smell them, tobacco, sweat, brass polish. The cold sun glinted on their buttons and buckles and their gaze was unblinking. He felt the smoke from the truck exhaust, warm against his bare legs. The truck engine sounded like an animal breathing very fast.

"Are you sure?" one of them said.

Now his anger was unwinding in him, flooding his arms and legs, filling his chest, making him big, making him strong, and he knew, positively knew, what war was about. "He's hiding. I can tell you where he is."

CHAPTER NINETEEN

Although Bert carried every detail of that moment for the rest of his life, he couldn't remember much of what followed, only that Donald must have protected them, for there were no repercussions as far as the family was concerned. They were not involved in the enquiry or the court martial. There was mention of it in the newspaper. It seemed Donald let his officers think he had stolen everything found in the Geronimo bakehouse.

Of course, he wasn't stood up in front of a firing squad. He was mistaken about that. But in a way, his punishment was worse. The life was slowly drained out of him in a detention centre somewhere in the middle of the North Island, conditions so harsh that he got rheumatic fever and never fully recovered. Later Bert talked to other chaps who said it was worse than being in an enemy prisoner-of-war camp.

As for Betty, when Donald was arrested, her spirit died. She stopped playing sport, wouldn't eat, and got so pale that Mum took her to a doctor, who said she had anaemia. She was prescribed a dark red iron tonic and some tablets to help her sleep. Amazingly, she never guessed that Bert was responsible for Donald's capture. She assumed that the military police had extended their search to the old bakery and had discovered the trapdoor was unlocked. Betty blamed herself for not getting Donald to the South Island earlier. She really was in love with him.

Bert knew that it was not Donald he had betrayed, but his sister. Hers was more than a teenage crush. It was something near enough to permanent, and there was nothing Bert could do to undo the damage. The pain Betty had caused him was small compared with his regret. He lived with that regret every day, but didn't talk about it. Even when she was in hospital after the last stroke, unable to speak, trying to hold his hand, he couldn't tell her the truth.

Donald was interred until 1946, a year after the war ended. He and Betty were married in 1947, with fifteen-year-old Bert as best man at the wedding. But Donald's health was poor, he couldn't work, and Betty got a job in a fish-and-chip shop to earn a few shillings over his invalid's pension. They had no children.

Bert remembered his brother-in-law as ghostlike, silent, unsmiling. His softness had gone and nothing replaced it. He looked empty. When he wasn't asleep he was sitting in an armchair, staring at nothing, his lips occasionally moving as though he was tasting memories. He died of a heart attack in 1950. He was twenty-six.

Betty never remarried. She put all her energy into work, bought the fish-and-chip shop, turned it into a restaurant, bought other businesses in the postwar boom and made a lot of money. She was difficult to work for, though. Had a big turnover of staff.

Aunty Vi said the milk of human kindness turned sour in Betty's veins when Donald died, and there was no going back. She was right. Betty had died full of anger.

As for Meg, well, she became a nurse, and was engaged to be married when the wretched horse accident happened. That was something else Bert recalled clearly, although he had no memory of what was said at her funeral. All he knew now was that it had been a hot day and he was a young constable sweating in his uniform. There had been too many funerals since then. Eulogy after eulogy, hearse after hearse, and all those flowers smelling like death.

When Mack came back from the war, he and Vi got a ballot farm, raised sheep and five children.

The wooden leg didn't hinder Mack in the shearing shed. He was as strong as an ox. Liked his tipple, but so did Vi for that matter. They were happy, Bert thought. His parents liked to have holidays on their farm in those days when Dad was blind. Mack would come into town and pick them up in his new Vauxhall Cresta. Bert used to wonder how the wooden leg coped with the accelerator and brake. Somehow it did.

Of course, they were long gone now and he had lost contact with his cousins, although he'd heard that one of the boys had gone to live in Tokyo. Funny, the way things changed.

These days, Bert couldn't control the shaking in his right hand. He had knocked his tea over his paper and phone, and was having difficulty picking up the cup. But his great-grandson leaped forward and righted it for him, then went to the paper-towel roll on the bench and tore off a length. Bert wondered at his speed. Young people moved so quickly.

As Erueti mopped the table, he said again, "Please. Tell me about the Geronimo bakehouse. That is such an incredible name."

"Thank you, lad." Bert settled back in his chair. "There isn't much to tell."

The boy was nothing if not persistent. "Koro says it was big. Some story about a soldier hiding there during World War Two."

"Long ago," said Bert, shaking his head, "and much too complicated. I'll need time to write it all down." The truth was he was now feeling very tired, and wanted the boy to leave.

"That war was a blood bath," said Erueti. "Nanny's eldest brother was in the Maori Battalion. He came home, but two of his cousins didn't. They were buried in France. Sixteen years later our people went over to bring their bodies back to their own land."

"That's nice," murmured Bert.

The boy stood straight and squeezed the tea-soaked paper towel. "Excuse me, Great-grandfather. 'Nice' is a pakeha word and has nothing to do with it. It was tikanga, the only right thing to do." He hesitated and looked at the sodden ball in his hands. "Sorry. I shouldn't have said that. I realise you don't know." He put the paper in the rubbish tin.

"Maybe I don't know," said Bert. "But I do know something about war. And we've had plenty since. There was the Korean War, the Vietnam War, Operation Desert Storm, Iraq, Afghanistan, Syria, Ukraine."

Erueti sat down. "Afghanistan is different. There is no choice. We need to stop the atrocities. I have a cousin who's a chopper pilot over there. Sure, we worry about him. But we have to do something to change a brutal feudal system!"

Bert wanted to say, "Who says it's brutal?" and "You think war isn't atrocity?" But the boy had a sweet face, and there was something about him that made Bert feel he was looking into an old mirror. He remembered how he had crouched behind the barbed wire at Lyall Bay beach, pretending to kill imaginary German and Japanese soldiers. Back then he couldn't wait to enlist and become a gunner. He scratched his head. The year before Shirley died, they went to Japan to see the cherry blossom. Jolly nice people. Very polite.

Now he was feeling very, very tired. Some words rose out of nowhere and tumbled out of his mouth. "It doesn't matter what side you are on, lad, everyone killed in a war is someone's child."

It didn't mean anything to the boy, who was looking at his watch. Oh, is that the time? He had to meet his grandfather and get to the airport. Sorry. Goodbye, Great-grandfather. He came over, shook Bert's hand and did that Maori thing, foreheads pressed together, but he also kissed Bert's cheek, which was very nice. He looked so young, full mouth, slightly girlish, reminding him of the other one, just a kid really, hiding dead-scared in the old bakery.

When his great-grandson left, Bert went to sleep in his chair. He awoke suddenly, thinking he had overslept and missed his sister's funeral. Then he remembered, no, he had been to the church and come home early, walking. Someone he knew had offered him a lift, but he had refused because he couldn't remember the fellow's name. He moved in the chair and saw that there was a letter in his lap, two sheets of creased paper with a long list of something. He didn't put on his reading glasses. It'd be a census letter, or some kind of marketing research. He folded the pages, put them on the table, then picked up the remote to switch on the six o'clock news.

THE END